CAN'T WAIT TO SEE MY FRIEND JOHNNY

MITZI MILES

MMK BOOKS

2022 MMK Books

Copyright © 2022 by Mitzi Miles-Kubota

Book Design and Cover art © Mitzi Miles-Kubota

All rights reserved.

Published in the United States by MMK Books

PUBLISHER'S NOTE

LIBRARY OF CONGRESS CATALOGING-IN-PUBLICATION DATA

Miles-Kubota, Mitzi

Can't Wait To See My Friend Johnny

ISBN 979-8-9862958-0-0

Fiction—20th century—Crime—Humor

Set in Bodoni 72

Dedicated to the memory of Lucia Berlin
with love and respect

Love and gratitude always
to Ron and Ivan, my main men

Chapter 1

Getting this door to lock is an awful lot like fishing: stand in the perfect spot, hold your mouth just right, give it a little English and know that whatever you're fishing for'll keep slipping away. Sometimes I give it all the English I have plus a dozen choice words. Forget begging–tried that, too. My days–anyone's days–are long enough without ending in a battle against worn out metal junk. More often than I'd like to, I just leave the damn door unlocked. Cross my fingers and hope some Lake Street bum doesn't turn my office into his boudoir overnight. Again.

Naturally, tonight is one of those cranky times. The lock's innards aren't biting. I've got places to go, people to see. Not really. I'm just pissed about freezing in the hallway my landlord's too cheap to heat and too cheap to light, jiggling my key in a chintzy lock he's too cheap to replace. A year and a half in this crappy office has brought me lots of work from the rightfully wronged spouses and business partners and insurance scammers, and my war with this doorknob has added a ton of charming new combinations of old, favorite obscenities to my vocabulary.

Friday night. There's nowhere I'm in a hurry to be. Wouldn't know a hot date if one bit me. And I'm a catch, I hear. My own boss, my own money. Okay-looking red-head under 30, five feet of pure muscle (ha, ha). Got a sweet '67

GTO all tricked out. I'm even sorta, kinda easy to get along with.

Problem? Reno. 1973. Under the influence of the disco craze, has even *more* fake razzle-dazzle than its usual self, and you have to go a long way to out-glitz a casino town for sequins and beads. Disco's bad polyester, bad hairdos, and bad music look to me like a direct rip-off of our trademark, tacky lounge acts. Disco's questionable style multiplied by a thousand because of this being Reno? Who needs a man who's more sparkly than her? That means no more decoration than the pearl snaps on a Western shirt. Am I too simple for the 70s?

And I know, I know: I shouldn't bag on our casinos. Casinos are Nevada. Plain and simple. Nowhere else in America has them. We are it. What else are you going to do in a wasteland of sand? Build playgrounds. But for Nevada natives like me? They're just one small part of a whole lot bigger landscape.

I like the hovering smell of booze and cigarette smoke as much as the next guy. Clanking mechanical works and ringing bells of the one-armed bandits are like background music. It's cute to see the little old ladies from Sacramento, with their white-gloved fingers black from all the nickels carrying their plastic change buckets from machine to machine looking for their jackpot score. Slot machines take up most of the floor in a casino, just for them. The noise is hypnotic. Roulette wheels whirring. Loudspeaker announcements. The throne of the keno ticket writers and their fancy brushwork in the center of it all. Dignified pitbosses and dealers in black and white wear ties and serious expressions. Black and white is the mark of the casino worker. There's even a shop called House of Black and White on First Street in Reno. The one stop source for everything you need. Unless you're a cocktail waitress, a showgirl, or a coffeeshop waitress. They get uniforms or costumes. And weekly weigh-ins. And gropings.

Lounge acts: Burnouts, never-wases, almost-wases covering everyone else's songs in big haired, sequined, used up splendor. The smaller the casino, the more tired the lounge act. Personally, they're my favorite part of a casino. They're really, really bad and really, really don't give a shit. The introduction of the rhythm machine has made the whole spectacle even more funny while the entertainer runs through a bunch of thumps to get to the right one. Electric keyboards likewise have jazzed up the stages. I swear those things can sound like any instrument. It's amazing.

But it's still background noise. What the locals see and what the customers experience are two completely different things. If you work in one, it's just a job—you do it and go home. If you live here, casinos are great places for cheap drinks and food; cashing paychecks (no questions asked (and you get to spin the big wheel—always good for at least a free drink toke, sometimes a hundred bucks); or finding a safe, clean bathroom. Generally speaking, locals only do the "casino thing" if they have company from out of town. Being a tour guide for someone excited about the opportunity to lose a bunch of money is an easy way to keep them entertained. They think they're getting the royal treatment while we know we're avoiding cooking and cleaning up and mindless chit-chatting. Who wouldn't rather have an all you can eat buffet than dried out chicken, canned beans, and lumpy mashed potatoes at your host's house?

Mostly, locals stay off The Strip—Virginia Street, as we call it. The Reno Arch, topped with a Sputnik-looking adornment, welcomes you to The Biggest Little City in the World. The Arch crosses Virginia Street right where the train tracks cross, too. When train comes, it blocks traffic in both direction for however long it takes to pass by. You can tell how long a train headed west will be by the number of engines hooked together to haul it over the Sierras. Three or more? Settle in. You're stuck for a while. Then as you're watching it go by, right in the middle there might be a couple more engines. Now you sit longer. There's always talk of lowering the tracks under or building a bridge over, but it never gets done. Plans get buried under politics, so visitors and locals alike sit and wait.

Seriously, most of our lives are lived around the edges of the casino world. There are some unfortunates whose love of booze or gambling gets the best of them. Booze mostly. It's cheap and easy to come by. Gambling by locals is almost looked down upon. We wonder how anyone could be that stupid. We know people lose and lose every day. That's why casinos are bigger, fancier, and have better food than the rest of us. They don't exist to pay out; they exist to take in. It's simple. We all appreciate that fact it when it comes time to pay property taxes which are practically nothing because of gambling money. Also: no state income tax. Definitely a bonus for living in their shadow. But if the gambling bug gets you, you can go down the tubes but fast. And take your family with you. I went to school with kids like that. They didn't look so good.

Divorce makes Nevada different, too. The state has made a damn nice business out of both marriage and divorce. You can get a license and get married any time, any day. Pick a chapel, any chapel. Get married in shorts and a t-shirt, drunk to your eyeballs. You're an adult. Divorce? Takes a little longer but not much. Six weeks at a dude ranch for out-of-towners looking to untie the knot. Comfy places. Homey. Then toss that ring into the Truckee River. Tradition. Locals-wise, divorce is common. Even multiple divorces. Growing up, kids like me were odd balls because we still had our original parents, most had a step-family or step-families. Different last names living under the same roof. No one thought anything of it. Same as knowing that the dinner show at Harrah's is family friendly and the cocktail show is topless. Same show but with boobs or without. Didn't think anything of it.

Or of the fact that whorehouses existed. I was 21 before I ever heard one called a "brothel." They were whorehouses or cathouses. We knew they were there and what they were for before we were out of grade school. Bunny Ranch, Mom's, Mustang, names we knew same as Safeway or Woolworth. Businesses. They were hidden out in the county. Sometimes you could catch a glimpse of the lights from the highway. That's as close as I ever got. Businesses that were none of my business . . . even if they were good for my business.

People call Reno "Sin City," though I prefer to name-call Vegas for that. Never been there. I hear it's big, and I know for a fact it's a different world. Reno people uniformly hate Vegas. Because it's there. Because it gets to make all the rules for the rest of the state because it's bigger. The state capitol might be Carson City, but Las Vegas makes the rules. Reno has a University of Nevada, Vegas has a University of Nevada. We had ours first, so there. It's flatter and uglier and hotter down there. The air conditioning in the casinos actually does that countryside a favor. Just a bit to the north of Vegas is the nuclear testing range, also, in my opinion, an additional ugliness. Signs along Highway 50 warn you to stay the fuck out of the range, and they will send the MPs to run your ass off if they catch you. And they always seem to. My friend Mona said she stopped once to get out of her car because she had dropped a burning cigarette between her legs, and she was wearing a brand-new leopard skin coat. Here they came in a cloud of dust. She saw the ciggy on the ground, stomped it out, jumped back in the car, and took off. The MPs just turned around and went back to whatever barracks or bunker or spaceship they were holed up in. It wouldn't have gone well if they'd caught her: she had a trunk full of Panama Red and a suitcase full of speed she was driving up from Mexico to Reno. A visit from the MPs would not have been convenient.

Speed. Amphetamines. The casino industry lives on it. Either you have to get revved up for your graveyard shift or you worked a shift, drank a shift, slept two hours, and it was time to go back. Plus, cocktail waitresses and showgirls need to maintain a certain weight. Limits are very strict. Their costumes are custom fitted and tight and expensive. They can't afford to get hungry. Speed. It's not too good for teeth and skin, but a girl's gotta do what a girl's gotta do. Thick makeup is for more than sex appeal. It hides the lines and dark circles. It's part of the costume.

This is our world — one that is completely unique in the United States. We don't apologize. We don't explain. If you don't like it, don't come. What Nevadans are willing to accept as normal is a far cry from everywhere else. We still go to school, church, the beauty parlor, the playground. We know that how we need to live destroys a lot of lives — ours and our visitors. You *have* to be tough. You *have* to be honest with yourself. You *have* to know that living in this fantasy land that was built to make money from weakness and boredom and addiction and a longing for the excitement of being bad doesn't mean you have to give in to it. It's a show. It's like a huge play where one side knows its part down pat, and the other can pretend to be whatever it wants for a few hours or days. You can't forget what side you're on. To get lost in the fantasy is deadly for a local. If you lose YOU, there are too many ways not to recover.

My point is: Don't expect much from me about casinos. I've worked in them, I love an occasional seafood buffet, but other than that they're just landscape.

Anywho, at the moment I have bigger fish to fry. The damn door won't lock. I pay my rent, seems like I could expect a minimum of security.

Granted when I signed up for this place, I jumped the gun a little. Should have looked at the big picture more carefully and not let myself be intoxicated at the idea of my name on an old-time, frosted glass door. Just like a detective movie. Should have woken up and smelled the patchouli. I'm not the only tenant on the third floor, but I am the only new tenant in this whole building since '66. And the only one actually using her office for an office rather than crash pad. And certainly the only one paying her rent the fifth of every month on the dot. The bottom floor here is taken up entirely by the King-Hi Jewelry and Loan. The second floor is occupied by an assortment of small-time businesses, a few of them legal. Notaries, life insurance, janitorial, answering services. I went around and introduced myself when I first moved in. Handed out cards. Got a whole lot of nothing for my trouble. Not many smiles, no offers of overbrewed coffee. Welcome to me.

Among the third floor's many aggravations are the long-haired, hippie artist types who have camped out—and I do mean camped out—in their so-called "studio spaces" for years and who my landlord—that cheap sumbitch Felix Belaustegui—got stuck with along with this lemon of a building. He bought the place from one of the resident artists who turned out to be a wheeler-dealer in sheep's clothing—a convert to capitalism—whose farewell to bohemia was pocketing a shitload of money and protecting his own with free five year leases. Then he abandoned them and their ideals of communalism and poverty for a groovy spot on Kauai. Felix figured he could run the artists off by messing with the utilities from time to time. Didn't bother them—I could have told him. They were either too stoned to care or stayed in bed. Collectively. I, on the other hand, griped, and continue to gripe, like hell. Serves the greedy bastard right. But, dammit, I wish I'd not been lured by that damn frosted glass window. Who do I think I am? Sam Spade?

There are good and bad parts of the tenant situation. A bad part for me is that Felix can't get rid of them for three more years, but the good part is that I love to watch him hate them. Another bad part for me is that I share the floor with their bad housekeeping and their vices and aromas, but a good part is that they do their thing and I do mine. No interactions are my favorite kind of interactions.

I'm about to give up on the lock and split off when the toothless interior miraculously clatters into place. I push against the door with my shoulder, double checking like my mother used to do. Habit. Drop the keys into my coat pocket and take out a pack of Luckies but no lighter. Now I go on a hunt between pants pockets and my way overfilled shoulder bag. The lip-end of my cigarette is waterlogged by the time I scrounge my Zippo out from under all the stuff I think I need to carry around in my bag.

I take a long drag and with my coat sleeve polish my gold-leafed name on the glass. "Flack Murrow" in an arc and "Investigations" in a straight line underneath. Had the same design, only bigger, painted on my middle window facing Center Street. It's a beautiful arched piece of glass. Not many people bother to look up this high, but in the late afternoons, I get to enjoy the way those big letters cast the shadow of my name backward across my office floor.

Putting "Investigations" after my name means a lot of things and practically nothing. It means I had the twenty-five bucks for a business license—which is the practically nothing part—the part paying customers don't realize about the snoops they hire: you don't have to do shit to get a p.i. license, just cough up the dough. There are a ton of shady operators out there. I pride myself on not being one of them. I take on the work I want—I have a decent knack for steering clear of flakes and fakers—and I'm my own boss, I can say no to whoever I want. That's a big deal for me. Also, Flack Murrow Investigations looks cool in gold. Totally makes up for my low-life neighbors; the hike up two fights of rickety stairs; the lousy street parking situation; Felix; walls the gray-green of an insane asylum; carpet worn down to the jute; Felix; and the sleazy King-Hi Jewelry and Loan on the ground floor. And then there's Felix.

Once I quit making a bunch of noise locking up and swearing, it dawns on me that the building's way quieter than usual. Even this late there's generally acid rock or whiny sitar music and a cloud of weed smoke and incense swirling around. Instead, it's pin-drop still and non-aromatic. Wait, that usually means there's an important Dead concert somewhere. Sounds quiet outside, too. I don't hear much happening on Center Street. No sirens or drunken hoots, tires screeching. The only thing moving besides me are the pink and green neon lights of the Club Cal Neva flashing through my office windows from across the street and coloring up a little bit of the dim hallway. Weird.

I don't like weirdness.

I flick a long ash onto Felix's "carpet," turn to get the hell out of the creepy place, and step right into a tall someone standing behind me. He grabs me by the shoulders, turns me back around and mashes me up against the door, the side of my face squished against the cold glass. A boozy-smelling hand covers my mouth and boozier breath slurs in my ear.

"Open it."

I jingle my keys so whoever's got me pinned can see that I'm cooperating. I take a few stabs at the keyhole. With the fumes in my face and the weight of the stranger pressing against me, I'm not my usual graceful self. And, of course, there's the general lack of mechanical cooperation I just told you about.

"Hurry up," he growls.

I nod. I'm doing what he wants. The lock releases, and I turn the knob fast, letting door swing wide so it bangs off the inside wall as the drunken stranger and I fall through the opening. I squirm out from under him and dive over my desk. He gets up to his hands and knees unsteadily and unfolds himself to a standing position. By this time, I have a bead on his head with my .357 – the lovely Colt Python willed to me by my Great-aunt Ruth. I cross the room, flip on the fluorescents. He's wearing a tan trench coat. Not a flasher-style one, all rumpled and looking like it was slept in. This one fits well and looks like it might have just come from the cleaners. His hair is dark and long, but in a neat ponytail at his neck though a few wild strands are sticking out here and there. Bellbottom, hip hugger Levis. Paisley print dress shirt, open down the front. A huge gold Italian horn hangs from a thick gold chain against the black hairs on his chest. Platform Beatle boots. Bright blue. The way he squints from the light and his mouth hangs open from being drunk, it's hard to say what his face looks like. Clean-shaven white guy is about all I can tell.

"Pockets," I command. "Empty them on the desk, you son of a bitch." He hesitates. "NOW, damn it or lose an ear and whatever's attached to it!"

I'm expecting the usual: guns, knives, grenades, but the guy proceeds to fill my desk with a bunch of worthless crap from all kinds of nooks and crannies in his clothing. A mostly-empty pint of whiskey, a pocket-size red notebook, a motel room key, a wallet, another wallet, a garter, wadded Keno tickets, another wallet, a rubber-banded stack of baseball cards, pack of Camels, and a tight roll of money bigger than my fist in the toe of a black fishnet stocking tied in a knot.

"That everything?" I asked. "Or is there a rabbit in there, too?"

"'s it," he says, but I cock back the hammer, go over, and pat him down anyway.

"Forgot something." I throw a Swiss Army knife, complete with the cute spoon and fork, onto the pile on my desk. Some desperado. I was hoping for an excuse to shoot him.

"Let's see who we have here." I gather up the wallets. He's swaying, touching his lower lip like he knows he's been naughty. "Take a load off," I tell him, waving him over to the wooden chair by my desk. Once seated, his head starts lolling around like there're no bones in his neck.

"Hey," I say, "you gonna be sick?" To which he nods. "Oh no, not in here you're not."

I poke the gun into his ribs and usher him fast down the hall to the john. We collide off a couple of walls getting there, and once inside he lets the party fly back out the way it went in. Since there're no windows in the john and only one way out, my way, I shut the door and leave him to wretch in private while I lean against the wall and do a mental inventory of any possible damage to my body. Wrist hurts a little. I hear him slump and know from the echo of his moans that he's now on his knees, draped over the porcelain buddha.

I've never heard anyone barf so long. In between heaves he's totally out of breath I figure he's not going to get too far, and I can slip back down the hall to make sure the Lucky Strike he knocked out of my hand hasn't set fire to this tinderbox. I find that it scorched a decent sized hole in the "carpet" then went out. Probably snuffed by the dirt it burnt its way down to. I swing into my office to get my lighter and hear sirens out front, a couple of them. I look out onto Center Street, thinking this may have something to do with my visitor. But it turns out to be an ambulance and a cop car pulling up in front of the Cal Neva. I go back down the hall to check up on my new friend. Haven't been gone more than a minute.

"You okay in there?" I ask, lighting up and spitting out a flake of tobacco. "Hey, asshole, I'm talking to you." Nothing.

I kick the door open. The smell is astounding. I flip on the light mostly to avoid stepping in puke. He's gone. I turn into the corridor, both hands steadying my gun. When I get to my office, I let the .357 look inside before I do. Nothing. No one. And all of his stuff — really the only thing about this guy that interests me — is right where we left it. That's when I hear a noise on the stairs, a noise bigger than one man could make. I run for the stairway, getting as far as the second floor landing. There's a struggle going on somewhere below me, and then I see just a flash of something, maybe a pant leg, jut into the stairwell on the next flight down followed by the crack of wood and the soft thud of falling bodies. It's too dark to tell how many people went down, but there's a lot of groaning and cussing on impact. I hear them drag themselves in the direction of the front door, and I sure as hell will let them go. Like I said, what I'm interested in is on my desk. I hear the aluminum doors to the street beat back and forth on their hinges, then it's just me and the weird quietness again.

I retreat in the direction of my office, ears and eyes peeled now for other unwanted guests. Once inside, I close the door and struggle the lock into place. Cross over to the window to take another glance at the activities on Center Street. The ambulance is still out there—its red lights circling, making it look like someone hit the jackpot. Then out on the corner, I see two men struggling to hold up a guy who keeps slipping out of their arms and flopping down to the sidewalk. The one falling down is wearing a tan trench coat. My uninvited guests. I pull the stained, yellow shades down over the three big windows facing the street. Open the bottom drawer of my desk and take out a fifth of Beam and a purple aluminum tumbler.

Pour the tumbler about one-quarter full. Slug the bourbon down warm and straight, same way I like my men.

I light another Lucky, down another swig of Beam, and dig into the pile on my desk. Pretty harmless shit. I untie the knot in the stocking, and the bills curl open only slightly. They've been compressed in there a long time. All hundreds. A couple of grand and change, I'll estimate. Somebody's stake. Somebody's lucky rabbit's foot from the looks of things. Somebody who's been on a steady run of wins, playing on the house's money and not having to go into his stash. Respectable. I knot the wad back in its stocking.

Next, I empty the package of Camels—learned long ago always to check a cigarette pack. Sixteen smokes. I open my Swiss Army knife and dissect each of the cigs. Nothing. Disassemble the packaging. Nothing there either.

On to the three-inch stack of baseball cards. When I stretch the crisscrossed rubber bands, they literally disintegrate from age. There's nothing special about the first several cards – no rookies, no special issues or park freebies. Giants, a couple Dodgers, some Angels – a West Coast fan, National League mostly. Got to have a few out-of-towners: Indians, Yankees, Tigers, some variety. The cards have been banded this way a long time, they're all curled the same direction at the corners and indented in the same places by the rubber bands. Every card is placed with the fronts facing the same way. Not one upside down or backwards. I flip through a little faster. About an inch into the pile, I turn up a $100 chip from Crystal Bay Club and about a half an inch farther, a claim check from—small world!—King-Hi Jewelry and Loan dated four days ago.

Four days ago. I wonder how the hell that ticket got in there. It must have taken the patience of a saint – or someone clearly paranoid – to work that little strip of paper into the stack without breaking the bands. Why all the trouble over a pawn ticket? And it kills me that I could go downstairs to King-Hi this very minute and get whatever it is out of hock if I didn't think my little visitors might be back, lurking.

I spread out the baseball cards, but except for reading a couple of things I didn't know on Mickey Mantle's stats, there are no more surprises. I put the stack aside, stick the ticket in my back pocket, pour another shot of Beam, and tackle the three wallets. One's a Californian, Walter Osmond Petrosky. The clean-cut face on the driver's license is not the guy I'm looking for. In the other two wallets are Nevada licenses, and Nevada licenses have no pictures on them at all. They're just light blue scraps of paper with what looks like purple mimeograph printing on them. Underaged drinkers' tickets to paradise. You can no way get an accurate idea of a person's looks from a Nevada driver's license. Height/weight/ hair/eye descriptions of these two men weren't any help. Both Mr. Medium in coloring but a little taller than most. The god of private eyes isn't smiling on me.

I'm getting ready to dig a little deeper into the wallets' archives when the phone rings. Loud. Louder than usual because of the current state of weirdness. I let it ring four more times in order to compose myself and to unsettle the caller.

"Flack here."

"You Flack Murrow? Like on the window?" Trying to sound rough and tough.

"That's what I said."

"You ain't a guy?"

"You want to make a point or a date?"

"I – uh, well," this rocket scientist clears his throat and tries to get back to tough, "I got your boy here."

"I don't have a boy and if I did, I'd let you keep him. There're plenty."

"Listen, we followed him, okay? When he went up to see you, okay? He used to have something that we want. Now that something ain't on him."

"What something is it you're talking about?"

"You're probably looking right at it. I see your lights on up there."

This little piggie's still close by. "If it's your wallet, yeah, I am looking right at it."

"What?"

"I figured as much. Look, Mr. ...?"

"Nice try."

"Okay, Mr. Nice Try. It's past midnight, I'm missing the midweek rerun of *Creature Features* — which is the only reason I pay for t.v. cable — because I'm on the phone futzing with you. I got the contents of your buddy's pockets on my desk and of his stomach all over the john. Where do you prefer I start?"

The joker on the other end of the phone breathes out hard into my ear.

"Oooh, baby," I say.

"Cut the crap." There's a muffling at the other end as someone puts a hand over the mouthpiece. "We want our baseball cards back."

"Why? Will your mommy be mad if you lost them?"

"You got a smart mouth on you. Someday you're going get smart with the wrong guy."

"Guess you're not him, huh?"

"Shit."

"It's baseball cards you're after? Baseball cards, baseball cards. Haven't seen them."

"I think ... fuck it ... I think what I'm after is *you*." And the phone goes dead.

"Uh-oh," I say. Always push them just a little too far, Flack. I scoop the drunk's stuff off of the desk and into my shoulder bag which is already crammed too full of stuff. Lay my .357 on top of it all. Hell, this is going to be heavy to run with. I sling the shoulder strap diagonally across my body, let the bag hang to the back. I head for the door, jiggle the son of a bitch open, turn out the office lights, and split. No time to lock up. In the hall, I waddle under the weight of my bag. Foot-long leather fringe and glass beads smack and clatter against the backs of my legs. Perfect attire for a silent getaway. With the pole, I break out the few remaining light bulbs in the hall that work, then use it as a cane to feel side to side in the gloom, down and around the corner. I hear the aluminum doors swing downstairs and men whispering. Long rays from flashlights beam around the walls in the stairwell.

Shit. They're coming up fast. I start moving away from the sounds and lights—and that means away from the stairs and the street door and down a dark hallway, which in the months I've been here, I never bothered to check out. I have no idea what I'm coming up to. There could be a way out two feet or fifty yards from me. It's nearly pitch dark. I try doorknobs on both sides of the hallway. Since when do hippie peaceniks lock their doors?

I know I'm missing one hiding place after another, thrashing around in the dark. Sounds like the goons behind me have gone into my office. I hear them swearing, tearing the place apart. Won't take them long to realize that what they're looking for is not where they expect it to be. But from the sounds of things falling and breaking, they'll take their search to lengths that are a bit more than necessary or practical. Handy thing about pushing men til they're good and pissed off: they waste a ton energy on their tantrums.

I take my lighter out of my coat pocket and risk the possibility that they might see the little flame in order for me to see where the hell I am. Almost at the dead-end of the corridor. Nothing but closed, glass-fronted doors on both sides. Hardly a glimmer of light except for mine until the lighter overheats and burns my fingers. I blow on the metal to cool it off. When I light it again, I see my old familiar friend: the door marked "Ladies" which I push open and go through. I have only a few seconds to case the joint for a purpose other than peeing. I'm in the little lounge area that must have been cute in its day. Stained and peeling pink and white stripe wallpaper; a crooked, gold-framed mirror with broken glass, a formica counter, and a wooden chair. I know through that swinging door there a shitter and a sink that's been leaking since the fifties. I try to budge the window that turns out to be painted over and painted shut. Oh goodie. I'm trapped like a rat, and my fingers are burning again.

"Shit."

I pull the little string on the bare lightbulb in a broken ceramic fixture above the broken mirror, and about 20 watts of spiderweb-y light barely brightens the room. Taking a look at myself in the mirror is fun. There are about six parts to my face like one of those op-art paintings. Pug nose, freckles, and a huge blob of curly red hair all randomly reflected in different pieces. I can tell you my eyes are green, but you'd never know it in this light. Not one of my better looks.

The wrecking crew down the hall seems to have stopped or maybe run out of things to throw. I think my heart might stop, too, but it bangs hard enough for me to wish it *would* so I could hear. Same with my damn annoying lungs, huffing away. Got to quit smoking. Right now, I gotta wait. When in doubt, wait.

After a century and a half go by, I hear a booming voice: "Police. Hold it."

What the hell are they doing here? At any rate, I'm relieved and I'm not relieved by the arrival of the cavalry. Questions. Reports. Reprimands about women being more careful downtown alone at night. The usual hoopla.

"I said freeze it, assholes! Don't you fucking move."

A sudden fluorescent glow brightens up the gap at the bottom of the ladies' room door.

"Don't shoot! Don't shoot!"

Shoot them, shoot them, I think. I tiptoe out to the corner where I can hear better and take a peek down the hall. There they are. My heroes Rodgers and Harney – or as I love to call them Rodgers and Hammerstein – facing the open door of my office, guns drawn. Rodgers, as big as a Chevy Suburban, is out in front with Harney/Hammerstein, my chubby little Volkswagen bug, about a yard behind him.

"Where's Flack?" says Rodgers.

"Uh, across the street. She's – uh – bringing back drinks."

"Yeah," says the other, higher-pitched voice.

"Like hell. Cuff them, Harney."

This seems like a good time to make my grand entrance. I unload my cargo in the ladies' room, planning to saunter onto the scene carrying only my cigarettes, lighter, and a tube of lipstick. Just a girl on a potty break.

"Hey, these creeps destroying private property?" I say, applying a fresh coat of ginger frost to my lips. I cap the lipstick and slide it into my front jeans' pocket. Prop one fist on my hip and wave an accusing finger at the two screw-ups. But I'm thinking to myself, where's the drunk? There are only two bozos. Should be three. I'm also trying not to appear too pissed off by the demolition of my office. "What have you boys been up to while Mommy was away? And look who else is here. What's up, boys in blue?"

"We was driving by and we saw these two running across the street, looking all nervous-like. When they came in here, we figured you might be in trouble."

"You're the best," I say. "I don't know how I'd have made it to the ripe, old age of twenty-eight without you."

"You know these hoods?" says Hammerstein, I mean, Harney as he cuffs the second man.

"I don't *know* them know them. We just met. They want me to locate their kid sister. Ain't that right, guys? But look what the hell they did while I was in the can. Didn't you two have mothers?"

I lean casually against the doorjamb and drink in the scene. The ransacked room. Two handcuffed, skinny speed-freaks trying to wipe their runny noses on their shoulders. Two meaty police officers wearing rehearsed, grim faces, their guns drawn.

"Think you could lighten up on my clients a bit, Rodgers?" I ask. "This could be bad for business if you know what I mean."

Rodgers and Hammerstein put their iron away, and the pathetic break-in artists look down at the floor.

"Come on, Hammerstein, take the cuffs off. They ain't going to do anything. They're scared shitless."

"Flack, it wouldn't be a good idea to ..."

"Hey, we're all friends here, right?" I give Rodgers and Harney the evil eye. Rodgers nods for his partner to take off the cuffs. The two losers rub their wrists and wipe their noses.

"Now, isn't that better?" I say. "Let's sit down and chat."

One of the thugs moves to sit in my chair. I tsk, tsk him over to one of the wooden numbers lying on its side where one of them had thrown it. The bad boys sit down. The cops stay standing by the door, each with his hand on his gun butt.

"Oh yeah, I forget you guys do nothing but sit all day," I say.

"Flack. . ." says Rodgers.

"I take it back," I say. "You do is walk from the car to the Winchell's every couple of hours."

Rodgers says, "What's going on here?"

"Boys will be boys. Got to watch them every second," I say. The speed freaks are looking at me like I'm Francis the Talking Mule. Never seen anything like this: a woman who's not begging for mercy or shaking in her boots or screaming for their immediate arrests.

"But they have made a helluva mess here," I say. "I think I'll press charges. That is, unless they'd like to discuss who referred them to me."

They look at each other in a panic. This whole business was supposed to go down much differently, probably with me lying in a pool of blood as one scenario.

"Who would like to go first?" I say. "How about you, Jim? Wasn't it Jim?" I wink at the pitiful sap.

"Uh, yeah. Jim."

"Well?"

He shifts around nervously. "I don't want to say."

"You?" I nod to his partner in crime. They look at each other and make their agreement.

"Nah, I don't want to say neither."

"Okay, then. You boys can take these idiots down to the station. I'm pressing charges. I'll follow. Fill out a formal complaint. Just give me a sec to get my pocketbook."

Rodgers and Hammerstein get busy re-handcuffing and rights-reading and don't even notice I leave the room to retrieve my bag. After all the time these guys have known me, they still cut me yards of she's-just-a-girl slack and I get away with murder — well, not yet but probably some day. I like them. We go way back. They were friends of Pops. And I think they like me okay, too, considering the problems I cause them. At least I keep their lives interesting. With oodles of "crime" being legal in Nevada, it's about the quietest place in America for the police. There's the usual drunks and speeders. But the juiciest goings-on kind of take care of themselves between interested parties, if you know what I mean. The only ones slow to catch on to how things work are the police force who have a mistaken idea about who's in charge.

Rodgers and Hammerstein and the punks were waiting on the sidewalk by the time I choose to make my appearance, trying not to look too weighted down by the ton of stuff I'm carrying.

"I'm ready, gentlemen," I say.

"Where's your car, Flack?" asks Harney.

"Oh, you don't need to worry about little ole me. I know my way to the station."

"See you in a few minutes then," says Rodgers. "And you *do* plan to show up this time, right?"

I give him my dutiful nod.

They cram the two losers into the back seat of the patrol car and turn east on Second headed for the cop shop. I walk a few blocks south on Center – lugging my bag of loot—and turn left at Mill. I found a great parking spot today. Smack in front of Mill Street Liquors, just inches beyond the first of the parking meters. I heave my bag of goodies over onto the passenger's seat, slide in behind the wheel of my GTO, and fire up the engine. A perfect purr. I whip a U-turn and head for Virginia Street—exactly the opposite direction of my date with police paperwork. I won't be too popular around there, but I can't be wasting time writing the story of my life while there is much more interesting entertainment sitting on the seat beside me. The police'll hold my buddies until at least ten tomorrow morning like they always do. By then I hope to have a better notion of what made my office the hottest spot in downtown Reno on a cold as hell Wednesday night in May.

But, damn, where's Mr. Trenchcoat?

Chapter 2

He comes to me like he was when he was little. When he looked up to his big sister, when I was the only one he knew he could count on. He's always wearing the same thing: that Spiderman sweatshirt I gave him on his tenth birthday, blue jeans with iron-on patches you can see the outlines of on both holey knees, too-big cowboy boots with curled up toes. He always looks like that. Carrot hair going any way it wants. Freckles splashed across his nose and cheeks. God, he's cute.

And he always just stands there with his arms hanging at his sides, toy pistols in each hand pointing down. Never speaks. Never moves. Only in the dream, it's like a camera which is me keeps moving back and back until I can't see him at all. And then he's gone. I know where. I put him there. For life. With possibility of parole, a small consolation. I thought he would only go down for a while — long enough to straighten him out. The court thought differently about how to handle a fifteen-year-old junkie who kills a cabbie behind Louis' Basque Corner. For a lousy seventy-five bucks, the prosecution claimed. My Timmy killed a man for a fix, they said. And I helped them find him. I did it because I thought it was the right thing to do and because they swore they'd go easy on him. I

26

hadn't talked to Timmy for a year since he'd run off from me. But I knew what he was up to, who he was hanging out with. So I turned him in, hoping to save his life. Because I loved him and nothing good could come out of where he was headed.

Turns out that cabbie was a twenty-two year old trouble child of an old-time Nevada ranching family – a spoiled brat with a long arrest sheet of violence and drug offenses who got his kicks out of slumming around trailer parks and shitty apartment complexes and dealing to kids—among other things Timmy told me he did with them. Whenever this upstanding citizen was in trouble his family could buy him all the representation and sympathy they needed to keep him out of court as often as possible and, on the off-chance of a conviction, get him out of jail in as short a time as possible. He and Timmy knew each other in ways I don't even want to think about. But try to make a court believe your word when your only chance is a newly-minted public defender and the victim's family owns the lawyer-brother of a US senator. Timmy told me killing the guy wasn't quite self-defense. He'd just decided that where the kinky appetites of this creep were concerned, enough was enough. But he did take the seventy-five dollars, and that and the cabbie's pedigree clinched it for the jury.

It became pretty obvious pretty fast how things were going to be for Timmy, and there was nothing I could do about any of it. I wasn't out of high school yet myself and flat broke from keeping him and me in food and shelter on a Harold's Club buss girl's wages, doing all I could to keep us together and out of foster homes. At the trial, it came out how he and I had been living for the past two years. The long story of things coming apart faster than I could fix them. Our parents were gone—died within six months of each other three years before. After that, we'd lived with another family, the Larsons, for a while but that didn't go so well. I decided I'd do anything to keep Timmy and me out of The System, and I all but died trying. The

System sent Timmy to reform school in Elko until he would turn eighteen then he'd be transferred to the Nevada State Prison in Carson City for possibly the rest of his life. Then they ordered me into a foster home. I never made it to the front door.

That wasn't the way it was supposed to work. My Pop always told us that the law protected the innocent. He didn't say what money could do to the equation. After I helped them get Timmy, I never again thought the law existed for anything but greed. Blind justice was bullshit. It's been thirteen years now and Timmy never has put me on his visitor list.

When I'm too tired to fight his face out of my mind, right when I give in to sleep, he's still the little boy I could tell about Mom and Pop, keep alive the idea of family in his mind. He's the little boy I stood up for against the rowdy Larson kids after Red and Edie took us in. Timmy wasn't much of a fighter. He was a studier. Never met another person who asked so many right questions so much of the time or could tell you everything about people just by watching them. Sweet, gentle, a personality I only wish I could have had, that was Timmy. Too good for what he and I ended up with in the world. The way he looks now in my dreams . . . How can no expression on a face say so much? Why can't I get him to hear me when I say I'm sorry? I hear myself say it or scream it or blubber it − his face never changes. Just that parade of freckles and the two guns by his side. Then I slide away but it looks like *he* goes back. Back, back, back into nothing. Away from me.

◊

I jolt awake, shaking and sweating as usual. Turn on the light by the bed, get re-acquainted with reality. Get back to being the Flack Murrow nobody messes with. No one needs to know that the thing that keeps me going is thinking that one of these days, I'll do some one good thing or enough things good so Timmy and all the damage that's seemed to follow me from my first breath on this planet will come to mean something or will simply let me alone. If I just try harder, work longer, the day's got to come when I can say, "Susan Anne, you can rest now. You're all paid up." And I can become a cream puff. A real pussycat with all my dues paid.

At least while I'm awake, there are no visions of Timmy. Awake, I can put him far enough out of my mind to get my job done. Jim Beam, Lucky Strikes, and the job are enough to want for now. And horseback riding. Sex if it's fairly anonymous and not too sweet. Trout fishing on the Truckee.

I light up a cigarette from the pack next to the lamp. Check the clock: 4:30. I haul my shoulder bag out from under the bed and empty out the contents. In my mad rush to leave my office before the goon squad showed up last night, I had dumped all those crumbled up Camels in there along with everything else. They make a terrible mess on my blankets. I brush what I can off onto the floor as fast as I can. I separate my stuff from the drunk's and take up dealing with the wallets I'd been ready to examine before being rudely interrupted a few hours ago.

Walter Theodore Petrosky, the Californian, had plans to get lucky: three spanking new condoms and a hundred and eighty bucks in his wallet. Pictures of his kids and one of his wife. Between his social security and A.A.A. cards back to back in one plastic photo sleeve, I find a full color beaver shot torn out of a magazine. A limp dick is looking forlornly at the beaver, so near yet so far. How sweet. I replace Petrosky's mementos in a semblance of order. Put his wallet in my bag. I'll stick in the mail to him tomorrow.

The first of the Nevada wallets belongs to Richard Thomas Sloane, a car salesman for Pozzi Motors in Carson City. Sitting on such a wad of business cards must give the guy a terrible backache, and there's not much more than those in the wallet. No kid faces. No old lady. Couple of credit cards, one gas, one expired. Twenty-two bucks. A folded up blank check from an account bearing his name only. Judging from the wear on the creases, the check was meant for use only in an emergency. Couple of fortune cookie fortunes: "You have a keen mind for success in business" and "The whole world is attracted to your magnetic personality." Words car salesmen run their lives by. No, this was not the man in my office last night. Mr. Sloane's getting his wallet mailed back, too.

Ah, ha. In the last one, a Louis Vuitton, I might add, I find a psychedelic-lettered ticket to a concert at the Fillmore. May 13th. Stoneground, Taj Mahal, and the Airplane. Coming up in a couple of days. There's also zero cash, a bent joint, and a $6.98 receipt from Sneed Hearn the head shop in Park Lane Mall. Here's a man definitely needs an extra wallet or two. Got to finance that trip to the City. It all adds up to someone looking to pay for wacky tobaccy and a tab or two.

You can read a man's character like a book from the contents of his wallet, same as a woman's by her purse, and as a general rule a man out picking up extras isn't holding wads in his bank account. My drunk is a contradiction in terms: a hippie in designer clothes? Tie dyed on the inside, snappy dresser on the outside. Name on the expired driver's license is Michael Robert Parker. Address is on "L" in Sparks — a neighborhood that's also a doesn't match with the money it would take to wear duds as fancy as his. Might be worth driving out there to see how and where old Mikey lives. If, given the 1970 expiration date, he's still living there.

Still, shit ain't matching up with Mr. Parker. Why would someone who could spend mucho dinero on clothes be stealing wallets? And not very good wallets either. Klepto? Maybe. A game? Maybe. The roll of cash wrapped in the stocking would go a long way to finance a lost weekend. Several lost weekends. What's with all the other crap?

5:15. My eyes are closing on their own. I don't want to sleep. Got to work. Got to know who brought me this hassle. Don't want to go ... don't want to ... Just as I'm headed down for the count, I see the red notebook. Pull it out from under the fishnet of money and flip the cover open. Cramped handwriting, precise and tiny. Some in pen, some in worn down pencil stub. Dates, places, little notes I'm too tired to try to read. I take another drink of bourbon straight from the bottle, and swear to myself this is the last cigarette of the day. I'll decide later if it's really the first of a new day. I flip quickly through every page in the book, blank or not, and turn up one interesting name and two phone numbers. Written big and underlined twice is Andrea LaPetite (my ass) and her number, and on another page all by itself is another number with a Lyon County prefix and no name. Got to give this guy credit for having consistent interests: undoubtedly these numbers will get you through to the same gritty—yet legal—underbelly. I'll give the rest of the notebook a closer look after I get a little sleep.

And, of course, I lied to myself about that last cigarette. At 8:30 a.m., I've already smoked three more out of a new pack. I'm showered and presentable in clean jeans and a Western shirt. I've spent two hours making a detailed inventory of the drunk's possessions on a yellow legal pad with ideas about each item's value, thinking that it might help me connect the dots. I've caught up with the news of yesterday in the morning *Journal* – more shit in Vietnam, more publicity for the new Ormsby House. And what about this Angela Davis chick? Nothing about a break-in at my place or a newsworthy medical emergency at the Cal Neva. I've had my pot of coffee and made a To Do list for the day. Stashed all of Mike's goodies except his notebook behind the cover of a hollowed-out Pioneer speaker I modified especially for such occasions. I tear my To

Do list out of the legal pad and slip the pad under a braided oval rug my kitchen table sits on.

By ten, I've left my padlocked Airstream, and I'm passing Moana Lane on my way north to the worse-for-wear, glitterless face that the Biggest Little City can't hide in the daylight. Got to get into town and see my two geniuses before the cops cut them loose. On no sleep and too much Mr. Beam, I don't think I'll be at my peak today. Picked a lousy time for those extra couple of shots of booze that never do what I've intended for them to do.

Chapter 3

"Those guys waited around for over an hour after they went off shift. You was supposed to sign a complaint."

Desk sergeants are all alike, just like the movies. He's leaning forward at me, elbows on the desk, fingers laced together. Elmer Grady. He's been sitting behind this desk all my life—the grizzly, sweetheart gatekeeper of the Reno Police Department. As usual he looks like he needs a shave but he also smells like half a gallon of Brut.

I wave my hand in front of my face. "God damn, Grady, you own stock in that stuff or something?"

"What stuff?"

"That perfume you're wearing."

"Oh, that. Like it?"

"About as much as I like getting stuck behind a semi lugging it up Spooner Summit on a hot day."

His face falls. "That bad, huh? Girlfriend. She give it to me."

"Girlfriend? Grady, you sly dog."

"Anniversary. Six months, believe it? She give me this shiny green bathrobe and a little basket of every kind of Brut stuff. Green's her favorite color." He rubs his hand over his cheek and gives it a sniff. Wrinkles up his nose. "Guess I did go a little overboard with it."

"A little, man. Hey, you still holding those goons Rodgers and Hammerstein partnered up with in my office last night?"

"Yeah, we got them. You was supposed to swear a complaint, Flack. Want me to get a uniform to take it down?"

"Nah. They're basically good boys — just need a couple lessons in manners. Can you let me see them please, Grady honey, love of my life?" I lean forward across the desk and bat my eyes at him, mostly blinking back tears from his fumes.

"Flack, you know I can't let you back there anymore. Orders."

"I promise I'll be good."

"Like last time? How such a little thing as yourself could bust a guy's jaw like that . . . You know what the captain said."

"But he's not here. I checked the sign-in board. He's down in Carson, no doubt polishing the department's image with the legislature. Not that it needs it. Reno P.D.'s a crackerjack operation if I've ever seen one. Top-notch. A-1. Now be a dear and let me see my slimeballs."

Grady looks around, craning his fat red neck to check who's behind him on both sides.

"Flack, I . . ."

"Pretty please?"

"Shucks," he says and comes out from behind his desk. He fidgets with the jail keys and keeps looking around and looking guilty. If he'd just learn to be cool, my dealings with the police department would go a lot smoother. He puts out his hand before we go in and I give him my gun. He locks up both of our guns in separate little vaults outside the jail door.

He leads me down the gray corridor to the holding cells. Must not have been much action anywhere in Reno but my office last night. Only eight little flies caught in the web. Three still passed out, slumped against the grimy walls. One's taking a crap and is quick to decide he's done once he sees me.

"There's mine." I motion toward the two men I recognized. Looks like Rodgers and Hammerstein gave them lesson number one in manners. The skinny blond of the pair's got an enormously swollen upper lip and his buddy, the acne victim, has some dried blood under his nose. I should be nicer to Rodgers and Harney. They've gotten my butt out of some tricky jams. I just can't help myself when it comes to them – it's like they have "softee" written across their foreheads when it comes to me. No matter what anybody says about me, about what happened after Pop died, they still back me up. I won't admit it to them, but I am grateful for that. Still doesn't mean I can't have a little fun pestering them, though, does it?

The blond and Mr. Clearasil interrupt their conversation, look over at me and do a double take. They're had. Just when they thought it was all going to blow over because the little missy would be too shook to make trouble for them. They get into an intense whispering match. The blond's pointing at me with a stubby cigarette while the zit farmer turns his back on me.

"You two. Hey! You sorry sons-a-bitches – sorry, Flack – get over here," Grady says with his hand on his empty holster.

The two make a few last agreements as they walk over to the bars and behind them I see the man who was crapping lick his lips at me. I flip him the bird next to my face on the side away from Grady and give him my look-that-kills. He grabs his crotch at me. I give him the inch sign. He starts toward us but thinks better of it. I could see to it that he got another night in the slam, easy.

"Grady, uh, I kind of need to talk to these guys alone. Could you do that for me? Come on, Grady. You're a saint. Ten minutes?"

He looks back toward the jail door, takes a deep breath. "I'll be right outside. Ten minutes, not a penny more." He walks out with his hand on his empty holster, and once outside, peers in through the little window in the door. I smile my good girl smile at him while I psyche myself up to speak with these boys in a language they'll understand.

"Okay, turds, let's start with the identity of your playmate last night."

Nothing.

"Let's try, who sent you?"

Nothing.

"How about what you were expecting to find in my office."

They're studying the floor.

"Lose your gum?" I ask, bending down and trying to look up into their faces. I lean against the opposite wall and light a Lucky. I can wait a bit — an uncomfortable silence works wonders sometimes. I blow smoke rings up at the ceiling. Poke the end of my cigarette through some of them. Look at my watch. Look over at Grady and see the back of his mostly bald head. One of the passed-out drunks comes to life and staggers to the can to take a very long piss. Everyone conscious in the cell looks over at him, impressed with his output. I'm impressed myself. I say, "Impressive," and stare back into my smoke.

I've obviously misjudged Heckle and Jeckle's tolerance for the silent treatment. Acne man's picking at his face. Blondy examines his fingernails.

"Let's see. You broke into my office, that's one count. You definitely trashed the place, that's two. I could come up with some cockamamie assault story, that'd be three, and I think I'll notice a few things missing when I start cleaning up the mess you guys made for a grand total of four unless I get real creative and come up with a few more. That ought to hold you losers for a good three or four months — more if I talk to the right people — and that's *unless* I decide to see about getting you sent down to the state pen for the luxury vacation you've always dreamed of. Now, who wants to start? Who was the dude you hauled off? And where is he?"

The blond one clears his throat a couple of times and says, "I gotta talk to Bi . . ., I mean, my partner here."

"I give you ten seconds." I hold the arm with my watch on it up to my face and start, "One, Mississippi. Two, Mississippi . . ."

They argue it out, pointing fingers at each other, until I announce their time is up and head toward the exit door.

"Wait. Wait!" yells Blondy. "We'll tell you whatever you want."

"Good idea. Names, yours for starters." They look at each other again. "Never mind. I'll get them from Grady. I'm going to go out on a limb and figure that what went on last night wasn't your brainstorm. Who sent you to my place? Who paid you?"

"We don't know," Blondy says. I turn to leave. He says real fast, "It was this slick Mexican-looking dude. Gave us a hundred bucks, each, to follow that guy and get back his . . . baseball cards."

I look as incredulous as I can. "Name."

"He didn't give it. Just said he'd meet us behind Landrums tonight at six to see if we got the cards yet."

"What's with the cards?"

"Dunno. For an easy — well, should have been easy — two hundred bucks, shit, what did we care?"

"How'd you know who had them?"

"The spick—I think the dude was a beaner, anyway—he pointed out who he wanted us to follow. We never seen the guy before. He just come in the place we hang out at on Fourth Street and asked us did we want to make some green. Said he'd hired the guy that morning to do some kind of work around his house, and the guy ripped him off for his cards."

"That all? Cards?"

They both look surprised. "Yeah. Just the cards."

Then Acne Man speaks up for the first time. "Yeah. Just the cards."

"Did you get them?"

"No, man, you probably know the dude didn't have shit on him. Not shit. That's why we went looking in your place only you didn't have shit neither."

"Whoever hired you isn't going to be too thrilled with your performance."

"No shit, man. Don't know what we're gonna tell him. We're gonna look stupid."

Acne says, "Yeah, stupid."

"Worried?"

"Fuck yeah. We already spent the money."

"Kind of between a rock and a hard place, aren't you?"

They agreed.

"Tell you what, I'm going to help you peckerheads out. I'll remind you you don't deserve this kindness considering how you screwed up my place and all. Lucky you didn't break my windows. Did you see them? Look good, don't they? Oh, didn't notice, huh? At any rate, I'm going to tell you what to tell your boss to get him off your case. Then you gentlemen become my friends for life, deal?"

The knotheads nod twice apiece.

"Goes like this: you followed the target to my office. That's Flack Murrow Investigations. Here's my card. We'll leave out the part about the threatening phone call you made to me. I wasn't there, got it? You boys wrestle, you fight, he gets away, you get him back. You get him down and you're about to go through his pockets when the cops show up. The guy takes the fire escape or flies out the window — whatever you want to make up here – and you two get popped which is true and you end up here all night which is also true and a tidy alibi to tell the Mexican. Got it so far?"

"Got it. But we still don't got the cards," says the brains of the outfit.

"True, but look where you ended up: a private investigator's office. Whatever your boss thinks of you as fuck-ups, he's going to be more interested in why you all ended up at my office in the first place. I think you'll be off the hook with this story, and me and your mark will be on. Savvy?"

Mr. Clearasil looks puzzled and starts to open his mouth.

"Don't, man, it'll just confuse you more," I say. "Just go with the story like I gave it to you. And here," I take two hundred dollar bills out of my bag and hand them to Blondy. No skin off my nose. I peeled them off of Mike's roll. "Give him back his cash. Make him more kindly disposed to leave you assholes alone."

Blondy takes the money and puts it in his left front pants pocket.

"Thanks, man," he says. "Thanks a lot. And we're bummed about fucking up your office."

"Yeah, really bummed," says the partner.

"Forget it. Just remember who your friends are. I'll get you cleared with Grady and you can split."

I go down the hall and bang on the door hard just to see Grady jump. I explain to him about my feelings for poor, misguided youth deserving a second chance, and he complains that the police department is not my personal warehouse for unsavory characters. After all, they had to feed them breakfast. Cost the taxpayers unnecessary money. I thank him for his generosity and understanding, he likes it when I do that (and I am half serious), and he says he'll cut the two men loose right after his coffee break. He goes to the locker and gets me my gun back. I kiss him on the cheek.

Gives me a great amount satisfaction to fork over someone else's money. But while I'm enjoying that small prank, I'm also getting a creepy feeling that out in the dark recesses of Center Street last night, there were more eyes than I thought watching my place. And although I don't tell them, the story Blondy and Acne Boy will be telling tonight behind Landrums is only going to make the man who hears it very, very angry.

Out on the sidewalk in front of the station, I stop to light a cigarette. Today's weather is sure a switch from yesterday: wind's still blowing but without the cold bite to it. It's a tease—won't be anything like summer here for another month—but I'll enjoy this little bit of warmth for what it is as long as it lasts. I take my time walking around to the parking lot in back of the station where "Police Vehicles Only" signs are posted all over the chainlink fence, and which is, of course, where I left my car. The slick little GTO stands out like a jewel beside those boats the cops drive.

A couple of uniforms I don't recognize—looks like they're younger than me—are admiring my car. Don't seem to mind, much less wonder, what it's doing there. They're just appreciating some fine American muscle. I stroll past them and unlock the door.

"Nice," one of them says.

"Thanks," I say.

"Husband's?"

"Pimp's."

"Oh. Well, have a nice day."

"Sure will."

I gun the engine and fishtail out of the lot onto First Street because they're still watching. Or maybe they're just momentarily glued to the pavement. One of them was kind of cute but me and my big mouth . . .

Something's bugging me—I mean besides this rotten hangover and my lack of sleep: what brought this particular mess to my door? How do I figure into this thing, other than that now I'm hooked out of sheer curiosity? Did Michael Q. Parker, the drunken fool, know about the pawn ticket he was carrying? If he did, I hate to tell him, but he missed King-Hi Jewelry and Loan by two floors. Talk about high. But I know I'm not seeing something here. How come I'm all of a sudden Miss Popularity with high caliber men of action like Blondy and the Acne Kid?

Back at my office building, I yank open the one door—the one that always gaps open about an inch—of the pair that constitute the grand entrance to the "executive suites," dreading having to straighten out the disaster that awaits me upstairs. I cross the ancient, gum-dotted linoleum and start to climb. At the first landing, I run into Felix with his hands on his head, glaring at the broken banister that's hanging into the stairwell by a thread. He's swearing the air thick in his version of English and a mighty sprinkling of what must be Basque.

"You!" he screams. "You! What happen here?"

"Gee, what did happen, Felix? You sit on it?" I light a cigarette, offer fat Felix the pack.

"I don' want you goddam cigarette, Murrow." He always calls me Murrow. Cute. "I wanna know what happen here."

"Let's see. The banister broke. Probably termites or army ants,or jungle rot. Probably going to get the rest of this place, too.

"Ha. Ha," is his retort. "Ever since you come here, nothing but trouble. The police. The fire department. Thieves. Murderers."

"*One* murderer. Only one so far. And she had a perfectly good excuse."

"I wan' you out. I wan' you pack up and out. End of month." He shakes his meaty finger in my face, his bushy black mustache drawn into a narrow clump over invisible lips. "This you doing. I know. And you gonna pay ME." He jabs himself in his barrel chest with his thumb. "Everyone tell me you trouble, but I say 'no, no, that nice little girl? She wanna play private eye? I give her a break. She gotta see she really wanna get married, settle down, don't wanna work.' And now this . . . Out!"

There he goes again. "Felix, you were itching to rent something, anything in this dump that you demanded I signed a lease, remember? You insisted: a two year lease. Now, if you try to throw me out without being able to positively put me at this location performing this act of destruction, I'm afraid I will have to sue for breach of contract and ask the judge for compensation in the sum of my remaining lease plus moving expenses. What is that? About twenty months left on my lease? Let's say in round figures a couple of grand?"

Felix turns brick red, his pointing finger frozen in mid-air, in mid-waggle. He huffs a couple of times, reaches his hands and eyes up to some god he's got nailed to the ceiling and rattles off what I figure are a whole lot of supplications for Basque poxes upon me.

"Dang, Felix. That was great. Does that mean I can stay?"

He pleads with his god again and kicks at the banister, a hunk of which falls into the lobby. Of course, he hurts his foot doing it, so it seems like the perfect time to remind him about the uncooperative lock on my office door. As far as that part of the conversation goes, it's really more of the same. Only louder. And he still says he's going to make me pay. I tell him I'll call my insurance and that seems to satisfy him. Yeah, like hell I'll call them. But it does look like I still have an office. For now. I'll piss him off bad enough someday that no amount of money will be too much to be rid of me. I call that an irresistible challenge, money or no.

I climb to my third floor digs and fish my key into the keyhole. But instead of putting up its usual fight, the door squeaks open from the slightest pressure. I back away from it and press against the wall on the left-hand side. I ease the door open with the side of my foot, look in, and oh boy, is Felix going to love this: there's Michael Quentin Parker, fully nude, sitting in my chair staring at the door, a veterinarian-sized syringe stuck in the crook of his purple arm.

This is weird.

I don't like weird.

Chapter 4

"Mommy, she's flacking me again!"

"Susan Anne, you stop that right now! How many times have I told you?"

The arms of my Pop's leather bomber jacket were my favorite weapon against Timmy. I'd zip up in Pop's jacket, pull my arms inside, and then whip my body left and right real fast, making the sleeves into slapping – Timmy called it "flacking" – leather bats. He couldn't get anywhere near me as long as I kept swinging. Which I could do until I got too dizzy. Drove him nuts. It was just one of those older sibling things, asserting my role as the big sister. He'd couldn't resist testing me. Naturally he'd get smacked a few times then run off crying for Mom. And being the dedicated brat that I was, when she'd come after me I'd try to outrun her. And I could—if I had time to get my arms out of flacking-mode. Without the balancing and pumping power of my arms to keep me upright and moving, ninety-nine percent of the time, I'd fall on my face and Mom would take the opportunity of my basically straitjacketed body to beat my butt with a pancake flipper. When that happened, Timmy "won." He'd jump around, chanting, "flack, flack, flack" with every smack from Mom.

Eventually "Flack" stuck as Timmy's name for me. From the time I was nine years old, almost everyone but my mother, my best friend, and a few stubborn schoolteachers called me Flack.

I still have Pop's jacket. Don't wear it much anymore. But it makes my closet smell like leather and just the faintest (unless I'm imagining things) hint of Canoe. I leave his jacket hanging right in the middle where I can see it and touch it every morning. All these years later, it's the only thing I own I'd hate to lose.

Chapter 5

Trapped. In my own office. A dead body sitting in my chair. Felix out there on the stairs, hating my guts. And my To Do list burning a hole in my pocket. Just how far I am from being at my peak this morning was debatable until I walked in on my buddy Mike who, granted, is in worse shape than me. But, his metallic stare, the dried foam at the corner of his mouth, the handsome shade of purple on his skin . . . I leave the room and contribute to last night's stench in the john. Doesn't happen to me often. I've seen and smelled worse. But, like I said, I'm not at my peak just now.

In the close quarters of the bathroom, I mince around on my tiptoes. If I put one foot under the sink and one near the opposite wall, I can straddle onto a couple of inches of puke-free floor. I douse a little water on my face at the sink and flush the toilet twice. There's a gray rag mop in the corner and about half a bottle of Mr. Clean on the water heater. I dump all of the yellow cleanser from the bottle into the toilet, plunge in the mop, and carefully back out into the hallway so I can spread good cheer from a safe distance over the walls, floors, and fixtures. My only use for housekeeping of any sort is to ensure that certain items or facts stay safely out of the limelight until it's useful for me to expose them. And there are times like the present when a bit of tidying can be good for the soul. Puts things into perspective. Clears the air, in a matter of speaking.

The few brain cells that are still with me this morning are in overdrive trying to keep up with the growing number of little and big details jumping out at me, some of which are or will be developing into real problems. All I need is for Felix—or the entire Reno Police Department for that matter—to blow a gasket on me from Flack-overload. I'd like to hold down on both the noise and the bad vibes from that happening at least until I get a better handle on the big picture. Maybe sloshing out a toilet is just a way to fake myself into believing I've made a teensy bit of progress. At this point, I may even chalk up washing my face as one point scored for the good guys.

Back in the office, I see Mike has waited patiently for my return. I ease in behind him—careful not to make contact—to roll up the window shades, get this place looking a little less gloomy. Yikes, it's bright out there. I go over and flip one of the knocked-down chairs into a sitting position, take a load off, and light a Lucky.

Trapped. I argue with myself momentarily about whether or not I need to take the closer look at Mike that until now I've felt too squeamish to take. After all, he *is* naked. The thought of wanting to see what a dead guy's got—or had—makes me feel sort of ghoulish, but how can I resist? Besides, who's going to know?

Yeah, he's naked, all right. All the way down. And, yeah, I take a look at "it." I suppose he was proud of this one, sizewise and pleasure-bent. What a pity all the good ones are taken . . . His legs show the raw signs of dragging and his upper arms are bruised. I won't need that degree I never got in nuclear physics to understand somebody's trying to send a message.

Can't figure what this has got to do with me but might as well assume the worst. I take a look under the desk, around Mike's chair. Nothing interesting or incriminating down there. The syringe in his arm is one of those metal-and-glass farm jobs that holds about a quart. There's dried residue about halfway up against the inside. White. I see no other needle marks on Mike's arms. This first hit was his last.

Trapped. A call to the general category "cops" would involve giving up far too much of what's left of my day. As it is, I'll be shuffling important To Do's from today's list onto tomorrow's because I'll be baby-sitting a nicely hung but uninvited corpse. I guess it's time to make The Call. At 11:30 a.m. on a Saturday, who might I be able to scare up at the station who knows me and loves me and won't take all of this the wrong way?

I wrap a couple of Kleenexes over the mouthpiece of the phone and dial the number.

"Reno Police Department." I think it's Grady.

"Detective Peterson please."

"Signed out til three. Can I help you, ma'am?"

Kind, sweet, helpful Grady. "How about Turley?"

"Swing shift."

"McMannis?"

"Yeah, he's back there. Who's calling?"

"Gladys Newbury."

"One moment, Mrs. Newbury."

While I hang on the line, I concentrate my fading energy on the view outside my windows. Try to rally some brain power by making up gritty stories about what could be going on behind each window of the Mapes Hotel. I'm so involved entertaining myself that without thinking, I accidentally sit back on the arm of my office chair. My butt makes contact with Mike's reptilian flesh, and I shoot up like a rocket right when McMannis clicks on.

"Detective McMannis." He says it with a calculated gruffness and perfected boredom that public servants must have to pass a test on to get their jobs—the tone that lets their callers know they're speaking now to someone very important, that important people resent being disturbed, and that the conversation from here on is going to be played according to the important person's gamebook.

"Bob." I unwrap the mouthpiece. "It's Flack."

He hesitates a second while he erases the image of Gladys Newbury, then eases up on his tough guy act. "Hey, how's every little thing, sweetheart?"

"Good. Real good. Plenty of business. Never a dull moment."

"How's the car running?"

"Great. How's Sharon?"

"Great. Big as a house. She's due in two weeks."

"How many does that make, eighteen or nineteen?"

McMannis laughs. "Only five, Flack. You should come by some time."

"I don't know. The way things work around your place, I'd be afraid of coming up pregnant just sitting on your furniture."

He laughs again. "Oh, *that's* how it happens." He keeps laughing – just one of those perpetually happy guys who loves his job and loves his wife and kids and lives to putter around the homestead on Sundays. How he ever made detective or, for that matter, stayed on the force for twelve years with an attitude like his is a mystery. I've never met anyone so hopelessly cheerful.

"Bob, I've got a problem."

"Oh? What else is new?"

"Believe me, it's a doozy. Could I get you to pay me a housecall? I'm in my office on Center. Know where it is?"

"Yeah, I think I can fit you in. What's the address again?"

I remind him and calculate that he'll show up in about fifteen minutes. Not much time to dream up a good story; I'll be winging it. I go out and sneak down the stairs to see if Felix is still lurking about. This building isn't the only rat hole the fat creep owns. I hope he's got other renters to bother today, other small businesses he can underserve besides mine, because it'd be best if he wasn't here when most of the on-duty cops in town show up. Then again—and this is going to sound dippy—I'm not totally convinced that in a weird way Felix hasn't got some kind of radar fine-tuned for catching me when I'm at my most in flagrante because this isn't the first time he's done it. It's very distracting to be worrying about when he might slither up behind me. Why the hell can't he just let his tenants run amok and his properties go down the tubes from the comfort of his Jacuzzi out on Franktown Road like a normal slumlord? That's where I'd do it from if I was one. And I'd be drinking a better brand of whiskey.

For kicks, I actually followed him out to his house one time. Damn if it wasn't on Franktown. Just wanted to see if the other half lives as well as we peons think. His house turned out to be a lily-white custom ranch model with a shake roof. I estimated six bedrooms, four baths. A brick barbeque pit and patio in the back. Built from the sweat of his tenants' brows. That's where Felix gets to spend his time scheming how *not* to put any money into his income properties. My feelings for Felix took a turn for the worst after checking out the classy digs my rent was paying for him to live in.

There's no Felix in sight, so I go back to my office and open the one window that works. While I was out, it'd gotten real stuffy in here. The sun is just beginning to slant in through all three windows and the place is warming up fast. In about half an hour, it'll hit ole Mike right on the back of the neck, which is going to make him, uh, unpleasant. Sun's one thing you can always count on in Nevada. About 498 days a year of vacant, blue sky and white sun. Still, no matter how long you live here, the weather always fools you: we can be up to our asses in snow in June or sunbathing on the banks of the Truckee in February. Today, the Stars and Stripes on the top of the Mapes is blowing straight east with barely a pause for a flutter but, like I said, it's not all that cold. Branches whipping around on the cottonwoods along the river are showing a faint springtime-like greenness—little bitty buds wanting to be leaves in a couple of weeks or a month. Those that the wind doesn't tear off, that is.

Now that I'm done making up stories about the Mapes while I wait, I take up daydreaming that I'm out riding—just me and Rockalee and the wind rolling tumbleweeds through the sagebrush. Jackrabbits zipping out of their hiding places. I'm out there hunkered into Pop's coat, hat pulled low over my eyes. Rockalee's long legs picking our way up the sunny side of Rattlesnake Mountain. I have a flask of Beam warming against my side. Or maybe a better dream, considering the condition of my head, is that I have a flask warming next to my tackle box on the riverbank near Mayberry Bridge while I flip a few flies at some rainbows. I always have good luck out at Mayberry. But instead of all the good stuff I pretend is happening, I'm in real life trapped inside on this beautiful day with a stiff who's lousier company than a used tea bag.

A polite tapping at the door has to be McMannis and instead of yelling for him to come on in like I normally would, I open the door a crack and slip into the corridor, demurely shutting the door behind me.

"What's up, Flack? Aren't you going to let me in? It's cold as heck out here. And dark." He glances around like something might jump out at us. The man's got good instincts for places.

"Bob, thanks for coming. Before we go in, I just want to say I realize you probably had better things to do today. Anyway, I hope this won't affect our friendship."

I push the door open and step aside. Bob's jaw drops.

"Let's go in," I suggest, and he follows me.

He automatically takes a pocket notebook and a pen out of his inside coat pocket and gives the shamblized room a quick look-around. He walks up to Mike. Looks him over, too.

"You touch him?"

"I know better than that."

"Sure, you do. Found him just like this?"

"Yep-er."

"Know how long he's been here?"

"I left around one in the morning. Just got back. Rodgers and Harney were here last night, too, and . . ."

"What were they doing here?"

I gesture at the condition of the room. "It's a long story."

"If this body wasn't the reason they were here, do you think we can skip that part of it?" He looks dismayed which is as unnatural an expression on him as a yoga position on a football player. "Dang, you had to call me . . ."

"What would you do, Bob? I'd start from 'A' with Joe Cop-off-the-Street."

"Yeah, yeah, you're right. Tell me what I need to know."

Here's the version I give him: "The deceased is Mike Parker. Said he lived on L in Sparks." (Let the police go and visit Mike's place. Takes an item off my To Do list.) "He was here last night. Business. We talked. He left. I get here this morning, and there you go."

"What'd he want?"

"Hired me to look for his sister-in-law. Ran out on her husband in Michigan. He said his brother said that the way she talked, she was in Nevada somewhere sowing her wild oats. Mike said sure, he'd help him out and being a man of good taste, he came to me. I was going to start looking for her today."

"He pay you?"

"Two hundred up front."

"Doesn't seem like a guy who'd have two hundred."

"Well, now maybe. He looked a lot better last night."

Bob leans over to make a closer inspection of the syringe. "Wonder what kind of thing that is."

"It's veterinary. You know, for horses and cows. To vaccinate them and stuff. I've seen them out at the stable where I keep Rockalee."

"Is that right? Hmm." McMannis straightens up and writes some notes in his book. "I gotta get forensics and the coroner and an investigating team down here. Let's see, what else? Oh, the stenographer to take your statement."

Think fast, Flack. "Mind if I make my statement down at the station? I think I've had all I can stand of Mike here's company, know what I mean?"

"Oh, sure, sure, Flack. I'm sorry. Yeah, why don't you do that down at the station?"

"Thanks, Bob. You'll stay in touch?"

"I'll do that, sure, sure. Don't worry, I'll handle everything here."

"I know you will." Music to my ears.

I pick up my bag and adjust my face to look properly mortified and humble as I head for the door. McMannis is on the phone setting up his afternoon. I give him a not completely simulated tired wave, which he returns absentmindedly while he talks. I go out and close the door softly behind me.

I bound down the stairs, digging around for my car keys, and before I can find them, I come up with the motel key I took from Mike last night. Room 312 at the Holiday Inn on Sixth Street. No accounting for taste in accommodations but you never know what can turn up in the most unlikely places. Could be Mike, could be a collector of baseball cards. And I have trouble behind me and hours to spend avoiding any further brushes with the law before my date to spy on the little meeting at Landrums. Apologies once again to the police department, and bringing criminals to justice aside, if room 312 turns out to be nothing more than an anonymous place to do some thinking and make a few phone calls, I could do worse on a Thursday afternoon.

Chapter 6

I whip the GTO into the Holiday Inn parking lot and pull into the far corner where two high cement retaining walls come together on the Interstate 80 side. Just in case anybody's looking. At that precise moment, a dust devil decides to tear across the pavement and gets bottled up in my hideaway, throwing a ton of sand and flying scraps of paper and weeds against my car's beautiful new magenta metal flake paintjob. It happens so fast, I don't see it coming, can't get my window rolled up in time. I close my eyes tight and wait for it to peter out. Damn things only last a few seconds, but they sure stir up the sand and garbage and crap. After it dies down, I cross my fingers and get out to inspect the damage. I'm chomping on sand, picking it out of my left ear, shaking it out of my hair. This baby tornado didn't pack much of a punch, thankfully, and everything on the car looks fine. I sprint for the lobby as paper and trash are still floating down to earth.

The only thing that makes sense about this Holiday Inn is that it's right next to the freeway. But even given that you can see the sign for miles, it's nowhere near a convenient off-ramp. You have to circle—pretty much blindly if you're not a local and if you're a local, why would you care?—through a dilapidated, 1940-ish neighborhood of little houses in bad need of paint with overgrown elms and cottonwoods full of widow-makers to get to the parking lot. Definitely wouldn't be my idea of a cool place to stay in Reno. I'd pick the Mapes or Harrah's or someplace on the main drag close to the action. This Holiday Inn is in a no man's land between Reno and Sparks—and the only place to go in Sparks is the "swingin'" John Ascuaga's Nugget. Surrounding the Holiday Inn are mongrel dogs guarding dead cars in dirt driveways—a more typical Nevada sight than the casinos are. I can't think why someone would pay any money at all for such a crappy, if accurately authentic, location. There's nothing to do for a half mile in either direction. And sure as hell nothing you'd want to look at. Nothing but dust storms, tumbleweeds, and grubby little kids.

A Do Not Disturb sign is hanging on the doorknob of 312. I check my watch; it's just after noon. A housekeeping cart's at the end of the hall and, having done the crappy job of motel maid myself once for a year and a half, I know it'll be a while before the maid gets this far. I tap on the door and say, "Maid." When I get no response, I open the door to 312 as quietly as I can and give the room a good listen before going inside. I leave the Do Not Disturb sign out.

Inside, it takes a second for my eyes to adjust to the curtained darkness where I can barely see the dim, white gleam of an unmade bed. I feel along the bathroom wall and find a light switch that turns on both the light and a real noisy fan which gives my empty stomach an adrenaline jolt. On the counter there's a toothbrush, a travel-sized tube of Pepsodent, a comb with long brown hairs trailing from it, a porno magazine of women with mammoth rear ends and the men who love them; a Mennen Speed Stick, and an open roll of Tums. I eat two of the Tums. In the wastebasket is an empty pint of Wild Turkey and two used rubbers.

I leave the bathroom light on and walk past the bed to open the curtains. Ouch, the sunlight hurts again. The window runs the full length and height of the wall behind a small round table and two chairs. The room has the usual appearance of temporary quarters: rumpled double bed; a two-drawer dresser with a black gym bag and assorted clothing strewn across it. There's a mirror bolted to the wall over the dresser, a t.v. bolted to the wall beside the mirror, a nightstand by the bed likewise bolted to the wall. And there's your standard-issue, faded print of a mediocre landscape over the bed, bolted through its fake wood frame to the wall. The gracious attention to detail you can expect at Holiday Inns.

The contents spilling out of the gym bag are a jumble of men's underwear, socks, wrinkled polyester slacks, and a paisley shirt made out of that slinky stuff that Hendrix made famous. An unopened bottle of Wild Turkey—drat, not my brand but in my condition I might make an exception. An overripe banana. A Gray Line sucker-bus ticket from/to Fresno, issued yesterday. Free drink tokes and lucky buck coupons from Harrah's, Harold's, and the Primadonna. And the topper: a kid's crayon drawing of Mommy, Daddy, the house, the sun, the doggie, "I love you daddy do you love me Tina." I read the tag on the gym bag. I'm in Walter Petrosky's home away from home. His Wild Turkey's looking mighty tempting right now.

I take the bottle by the neck and flop down on the bed. Fluff up the pillows behind my head, break the seal on the booze, and take a slightly nauseating swig that I know in a few minutes will make my boo-boo go away. What a trip: I'm lying in some strange man's unmade bed, drinking his booze, and I still have my clothes on. I've also got a claim check for a mystery item I'm dying to see in a pawn shop in a building that, because of a naked dead guy in my office, is swarming with police activity.

After one more medicinal swig and I cap the bottle and set it on the nightstand. It's time to check out Mike's phone numbers. If I'd buy myself a real purse someday, one with zipper compartments and pockets and whatnot, I could get myself organized and quit wasting valuable time rummaging through all the crap I insist on carrying with me, looking for that one item that always escapes to the very bottom. And I know what this raunchy old roughout pouch I lug around says about my personality, but I figure there're worse identities than being a slob. Takes me a while, but I find Mike's notebook without having to dump everything out. While I'm at it, I toss Petrosky's wallet onto the bed.

I flip through the notebook and find the phone numbers. Both long distance. And the notice on the phone says long distance calls must go through the hotel switchboard.

"Desk," comes the operator's voice.

"Hi. This is Mrs. Petrosky in 312," I say. "I'd like to make a long-distance call."

"It will be added to your bill," is the terse response.

"Oh, of course, I know that. We'll be happy to pay any charges."

She sighs audibly. "I can dial the number for you now." I must have disturbed her Harlequin romance-reading or fingernail-filing.

"Any chance I could dial it myself?"

"No, ma'am. Room phones are blocked. Only local calls go out direct."

I read Andrea LaPetite's number to the crabby broad who repeats it back to me twice. Then I wait while she horses around dialing it for me. I can hear her breathing on the line.

"You can hang up now. It's ringing."

"Sorry, hotel policy."

My ass. Looks like I've got myself a cowgirl at the switchboard. That's what I call them: cowgirls and cowboys.

They're a particular group of Nevadans who take the whole wild west, gunslinger code way too seriously into whatever petty domain they think they're in charge of. You run into cowgirls and cowboys who are, say, the bank tellers who demand that you go to the end of the line because your deposit slip's got the wrong date on it. Or you might meet one of these cowpokes at the laundromat: they have no trouble telling you that those four empty dryers have been staked out as their own, private possessions while they—and you—wait for their wash to finish, and God help you if you go near one of them. It's frontier justice reduced to its dumbest, but these folks are dead-serious about whatever stupid issue their knickers are in a twist over. Makes for some lively verbal, sometimes physical, exchanges. Fun if you've got the time and the inclination. I'm tapped out of inclination at the moment. Looks like "Desk" and I will be listening on together.

The words "Cottontail Ranch" ooze from the holes in the receiving end of my phone like some kind of thick, pink confection, and I picture the woman who has answered standing by a powder blue princess phone, winding the powder blue cord around a slender finger tipped with a long red nail. I picture her tiny toes with perfect red pedicures poking delicately from open-front, white satin mules. I picture . . .

Then I'm cut off. Brunhilde of the switchboard has curtailed my call and has the nerve to hang up on me. I call her back.

"Desk." Snottier.

"This is Mrs. Petrosky again. 312? My call was cut off." Temper, temper, Flack.

"Mrs. Petrosky, it is against hotel policy to permit customers to call . . . those places. We are not that kind of establishment."

"What kind of establishment would that be?"

"A . . . a . . . house of ill-repute."

This broad's full of surprises. Not only is she a cowgirl, she's one of those nincompoops who's probably lived here all her life and still has to pretend she's such a lady she can't call a whorehouse a whorehouse.

We live in the only state in the union with legalized prostitution. Our whorehouses buy business licenses, pay taxes, and a few have even been known to throw a pretty decent Christmas party for poor kids from time to time. Naturally, some other "legitimate" business—a casino or a strip bar that calls itself a restaurant—may be the front for any charitable work the brothels might be up to, but that's only so people like this cowgirl can maintain their dream world. Nobody will claim whoring Nevada style is a pleasant business. You've got your rotten apples and your little less rotten apples and there are few hearts of gold. But we live with these places, that's a fact. Girls put themselves through college or support their families for a few years. If they're smart or lucky they get out before the work does them in one way or another. When you think about it, though, whose work doesn't? All work you get paid for is a sort of prostitution if you think about it.

I look at my watch. Still early and my inclination to mess with her is stirring since Brunhilde of the Front Desk is not only a cowgirl but a cowgirl pretending to be a prude. Time for a little fun.

I say in all insincerity, "Is that what Cottontail Ranch is? And it sounded so cute! Like a nursery school. Oh my, I had no idea. My baby sister wrote this number in the first letter I've had from her since she ran away. No wonder she begged me not to tell Mother and Father." I don't have time for this, but Miss Andrea may know something I need to know. I launch into some brief boo-hooing, a couple of well-placed sniffles to see if I can move the immovable object. Brunhilde is loving this, I can tell. Good gossip for her to dish to her cronies over their Sunday brunch vodkas and orange juices.

"You poor, poor dear," she says, and a different colored ooze seeps into my ear. "Your sister is a . . .?"

I take another slug of Turkey and make my voice as tiny as a church mouse. "We haven't heard from her in eight months. And now she's, she's . . . Oh, I hate to think . . ." More booing and hooing.

"Gracious," says the she-devil. "I can't think of anything worse. Your own baby sister. How old is she?"

"Just seventeen. Just seventeen last week. Can't you please help me get through to her?"

"I'm sorry, Mrs. Petrosky. Those are the rules. You'll need to call from somewhere else."

"But between us girls . . .?"

"No, ma'am. I can't. I could be fired. This is a *family* place."

"Oh, yes. Of course. I'm terribly sorry to have bothered you." Bitch. "But could I ask you to please try one more number for me? It may be my only other hope of finding our Suzie."

"Is it another one of . . . those places?" She's pissed but nosy.

Sniffle, sniffle. "I have no way of knowing. Mother said it was on the last page of Suzie's diary, the day before she . . ." Sniffle, swig.

"Oh, the poor thing. What's the number?"

Wouldn't you know it? "Bunny Ranch." How come all of these places are named after tick-infested rodents? Whatever link there was between Mike and these brothels I'm thinking I don't want or need to know all that badly right now. Sure, "Ranch" may appear on just about every brothel d.b.a.—and it does give you sort of a livestock feel when you think about it— but there's not enough connection between that definition of "ranch" and the kind of real-ranch hardware Mike had stuck in his arm. Mike's o.d. is my dead end.

I've had all the fun I can have with my cowgirl and content myself to sit tight, nurse my hangover, and stare at the ceiling until I decide on my next move. And hey, maybe Petrosky'd show up with some good news for me. I refluff the pillows and flip idly through the red notebook, reading a bit here and there. Dates, places, numbers, addresses. Then I start to notice a couple of details that are not only close to home, they *are* home. Mixed in with a few unrelated scribblings is a play-by-play of my recent activities: the place where my trailer's parked now, my new office, my license plate number. The address of The Fireside Chat where I like to hang out if I feel like hanging out. Marjean's where I get my hair mowed. The place where I board my horse. Dates and times picking up from about five months ago. From just before I left my partnership situation in Sparks and went out on my own. Mike's been following me. And with his demise coming as it did on my stomping grounds, I'd bet big money that somebody new has taken up where he left off. So much for thinking no one's going to care where I am.

Creepy. Real creepy. How could he have been tailing me for that long and I never noticed? Me? The one who's been looking over her shoulder since she was twelve? And by a drunk like Mike? Drunk must not be his usual nature.

It's true. It's been a tough couple of months. I guess I must have been more distracted than I thought while I was making my move away from Recovery Specialists, Inc., and into business for myself. Breaking off from my old partners—the five of us who got fired from our security guard jobs at the Desert Diamond in '69 because of a slick little embezzling operation that a graveyard slot manager and one of the upstairs execs had going. And it turned out that it wasn't just them. It was big. We blew the whistle, but in the end we also took the fall.

With the five of us out of the way, the crooks went back to business as usual. Since we had the time on our hands, we set up a slick little operation of our own. To clear our names more than anything. When we joined forces, we brought them down like Davey did Goliath.

We ended the legal and illegal careers of some of the Desert Diamond Casino's most trusted managers and some of the executives, too. We won big in our wrongful termination suit, too. After it all came out in the papers, we had job offers pouring in from practically every casino in Nevada plus the Gaming Commission. But not wanting to risk another set up at another time down the line, we became Recovery Specialists, Inc., and our business boomed overnight.

We also won the stifling, constant presence of each other, which no one seemed to mind but me. Then the money got cushy and I got bored. Between those two things, I'm surprised I hung with Recovery Specialists as long as I did.

I had to get out. Had to get me some room to breathe. But here's the funny part about being bored by the easy money: hating lawyers the way I do, I stupidly let my partners structure our new company and, as fate would have it, when I decided to go, I lost practically every cent from my share of the settlement *and* had to sign a non-competition agreement. Like I wanted to keep doing what I was bored stiff doing. But I would have liked to have kept the money. What a sap! Like I said, it was a rough couple of months, and I'm just happy now to be free.

I light a cigarette and take another drink from the bottle. In the red notebook, I recognize some of my clients' license numbers. Addresses of two guys whose names I can't remember but who I'd spent nights with on separate occasions in March and April. I find out I'd stayed home on New Year's

Eve. I had. How many times I'd been to Waldenbooks. That I'd been to the dentist. That two weeks ago I'd had my car repainted from "sea green to metal flake ruby red." Poetic. The last entry was three days ago. Then for whatever reason, the tracking stopped.

I was trying to calm the hairs on the back of my neck when I hear quick, heavy footsteps in the hall. I scoot down to the end of the bed, my hand on the .357 inside my bag on my lap. A key slips into the lock and the door opens and I know that face from the driver's license.

"Walter," I say.

He staggers a few steps backward from fright, looks at the door and looks at me and looks at the door again.

"Hey, Walter, I found your wallet. And your other room key, in case you hadn't noticed." I keep my hand on the gun for now even though he looks plenty scared of me. His hair's a mess and his face is unshaven.

"You . . . you . . ." he stammers.

"Come on in, I won't bite." Given the sheepish way he inches into the room, I figure I won't be needing the gun. I take my hand out and stretch behind me to reach the Wild Turkey on the nightstand.

He comes into the room slowly and takes a good look at me — all five feet one and almost a hundred pounds of me (most of it hair) — and decides I don't look too dangerous, I guess. I offer him his own bottle and point to one of the chairs by the little round table. He sits obediently.

"Smoke?" I say, shaking two up out of the pack.

"Uh, I don't uh . . ."

"You mind?" I say before lighting up.

"No, go ahead." He uncaps the bottle with shaky hands and takes a long drink that makes him shiver. Amateur. Runs his hand over the stubble on his face then kind of sinks into himself with the bottle in his lap.

I blow smoke out of the corner of my mouth away from him. "Oh, before I forget. Here." I underhand his wallet to him and I swear the guy almost looks like he's going to cry. He gapes at it as if it's solid gold. Then he does start to cry.

"Hey, Walter. Man, get ahold of yourself. Everything's okay. You got your wallet back." He's wiping his nose with the back of his hand—the hand he's holding the bottle with, damn him—and he's going, "gii, gii, gii," like that, trying not to make too much noise and looking real silly trying to hold it in.

"I shouldn't of done it," he says after he gets it together a little. "I shouldn't never . . . Lorraine. What've I done?"

And I'm pretty sure I know and don't want to know, but he's going to have to tell me anyway before I'll get a chance to ask him about Mike.

He says, "I just wanted . . . I just wanted to . . . you know," he looks at me all disturbed, "have a little fun. I got this bonus, see, at work? I don't tell her. Lorraine, my wife. Next thing I know, I have a few beers and I'm on a bus coming up here. I just ran out . . ."

He starts up his "gii-ing" again. I smoke and wait. It's getting on to 1:30 by now. The next bit he'll confess to me will be the part about how long he's been married, how much he loves his wife, how he's never done anything like this before.

"I've been married almost fourteen years." See? "I love my wife. Have a picture of her right here."

He starts to open his wallet and I say, "Already seen it, Walt."

"Yeah," he says, getting all dreamy on me. "I got three kids."

"I know you do. Have another drink, you'll feel better."

He takes a huge gulp and shivers again, but he's getting calmer. "My wife, she don't . . . She isn't . . . We hardly ever . . . after the last kid come ."

"Yep."

"She just doesn't know how it is for a man." He looks me straight in the eye for the first time. "I had to, just this once. You know, with someone who didn't mean nothing to me? I figured I could just do my thing and go back home. Over and done with."

"Yep."

Pitiful souls like Walter never get through their heads that a pro will give you a lot of things, but your manhood back is not one of them. Ever. At that moment, he didn't care if I was listening or not. Men only care about getting off the hook when they act like this. He's spilling everything except the extra gory details of what I imagine went on in this bed that make me want to go home and bathe. I'll let him get his guilt trip out of his system, and get him to calm down enough to give me some information I can use.

He goes on, "When I got up this morning and the girl was gone and my wallet was gone, all I could think was, 'Oh my god, that girl, she ripped me off. On top of everything, how am I going to explain *this* to Lorraine?' I was plastered last night . . ." He cradles his long lost wallet. "I've been all over town today — everywhere I could remember going last night — trying to find it. And here you are," he looks at me like I'm something saintly, something not like a whore or a cheated-on wife. "I don't know how to thank you."

"It's mellow, Walt. Let's just forget it, man. You go home, keep your mouth shut, and enjoy the memories."

My forgiveness, or his impression of my forgiveness, puts him back in real man mode, and as we chit chat, he convinces himself that it was *his* idea not to spill his guts to Lorraine. He starts to smile, relax a little, the old manly confidence settling back into his loins.

I imagine the Petrosky household is like this: he's got a fairly new truck with big wheels (guys like him need that), and one of his kids isn't getting the braces he needs because

Walter says they can't afford them. Walt goes out honky-tonking every Friday after work with the guys because they're men and that's what men do. Has a garage full of tools, a cabinet full of firearms, plenty of beer, and his wife has to put a phone book under the couch where the leg's broken off and a blanket over where the stuffing's showing through. I'll wager his wife goes to the grocery store with a calculator because she only has a pitiful allowance she can spend and five mouths to feed. Piss on him and piss on all of those like him.

I look at my watch. "Okay, well, gotta go, but I wonder if I could ask you a couple of questions."

"Shoot, little lady," he says, stretching his legs out and crossing his sneakered feet on the bed. Much calmer now. Gruesome combination: guilt, confession, the perception of forgiveness. And Wild Turkey.

"You meet a guy by the name of Mike last night?"

"Mike? No, don't think so."

"Sharp dresser, over six feet, slicked-back black hair, tan overcoat?"

Walter thinks for a second, his face pales again. He puts his feet down. "Yeah, yeah, I ran into that guy in the Nevada Club. He's the one who fixed me up with that girl." He looks at first like the little-boy-caught-with-his-hand-in-the-cookie-jar but that gives way almost immediately to a leer as he recalls last night.

Yuck. "You guys talk about anything else?"

"Oh, um, I bought him a drink while we were waiting. Told him I was up from Fresno. The usual stuff."

"What'd he have to say?"

"Said he hadn't lived in Reno too long. Couple years. Said he did a little of this, a little of that for a living. Called it 'personal services.' Sort of like what he done for me, I guess. We walked over to the Cal Neva together and met up with that girl, Silky. Then it's like, I don't know what happened. All of a sudden, he's running out of the place. That's the last I seen of him."

"See anybody chasing him?"

"I was kind of busy at the time, if you know what I mean."

"Yeah, I guess you were." I get up and sling the strap of my bag over my shoulder. "Well, it's been a pleasure. Good luck, Walt."

He gets up unsteadily from the chair and comes toward me. "Hey, since we're here all alone," he pats the bed, "you wouldn't want to, uh . . .?"

I shove him back down onto his chair. "Goddam, you're absolutely right about that. No, I wouldn't. And here's a little prediction from me to you, Walt: Lorraine's going to find out, you know, what you did while you were here. Know how? You're going to tell her. You won't be able to stop yourself. You're going to want to see how she takes it–finding out what a big man she's married to, doing whatever the fuck he wants. And you know what? If she leaves you, takes the kids and adios-es, I hope it won't come as a real big surprise."

Walter's whole body is rigid with amazement, and I know from experience that he's not going to be able to think of a single thing to do or say for a couple of minutes.

"Pick your jaw up off the floor, Walt," I say with my back to him, walking toward the door. "You look like an idiot."

Chapter 7

I slam the door on the mess I've made of Walter's wild weekend and try to shake the scum out of my head. I hear him get up and stomp across the room. By the time he jerks the door open, I've got the Python in my hand, aimed in his direction.

"Don't even think about it," I say. "Wave bye-bye, Walt."

He just stands there staring. I twiddle the fingers of my left hand at him.

"I said, wave bye-bye."

He twiddles the fingers of his right hand at me.

"That's nice. Now, go inside and shut the door like a good boy."

He does. I hear a noise to my left and pivot quick, swinging the gun toward the sound. It's just the maid coming out of the room next door with an armload of dirty sheets. She drops them and puts her hands over her head.

"Oh," I say. "Sorry about that." I put the gun back in my bag and dig out my wallet. From where she is, she'll never know I'm flashing my old photo i.d. from the Desert Diamond. I've kept it all these years because it looks authentically law-like. Gotten me out of more than a few jams. I clear my throat and say in my deepest, I-mean-business-voice, "F.B.I.."

Holding my i.d. up high like they do on t.v. "Everything's fine. Under control. Go on about your business. No cause for alarm."

She lowers her hands, makes the sign of the cross. I pull myself up to my full, statuesque height and stride purposefully around the corner to the elevators. Push the down arrow button. Both elevators are on the ground floor, and I'm stranded waiting for one to come up.

I look out the window into the parking lot. The GTO's right where I left it. About six spaces away, there's a blue Ford pickup, next to that a U-Haul. This time of day I recall as being sort of dead time in the hotel business, customerwise. A little after two. Past check out time and not many people checking in yet. Most tourists are walking up and down Virginia Street with their white tubs of nickels and black-smudged fingers. A few who think they're cultured or the ones who have had to bring their kiddies along will be pretending to be interested in downtown Reno's historical architecture: the Riverside, the Mapes, the post office, the courthouse. Personally, my favorite things to look at downtown are the giant showgirl statues on the front of the Primadonna and the mural of the pioneers on the front of Harolds. If you consider that those are the high spots, it's pretty easy to figure out that Reno's not the greatest vacation spot for either the cultured or the kid-ed regardless of what the Chamber of Commerce tells you. You can run out of architecture to look at or things to entertain the family with downtown in about an hour. After that, you could end up sitting around the Holiday Inn in the middle of the afternoon. But for the moment, it's all quiet on the Sixth Street front.

Neither elevator has moved off "L." I poke the button a few more times. I take a quick peek around the corner at each end of the long hallway. The maid's gone into the room she was working on. Better be on my toes now that I know what's in the red notebook. While I'm looking for bad guys, one elevator dings and the sound makes me jump. The doors slide open.

A whole family — crying baby, bickering little girls in matching pink outfits, and haggard parents in seersucker shorts (didn't get the memo about May in Reno, brrrr) — spills from the elevator into the hall, and I move over against the opposite wall to escape the flood. The other elevator dings its arrival. A bellboy I can barely see over the top of all the suitcases and assorted toys and baby furniture he's pushing on a cart maneuvers to make the turn, trailing after The Brady Bunch with all the domestic necessities it takes to make a hotel room a home. I hold the door open for him and smile over at Mrs. who gives me a "save me from this hell" look as she herds her grouchy daughters around the corner. The baby's in a real screaming fit somewhere down the hall in Daddy's arms. With them out of the way, I get in and press the "L" button five or six times to hurry the damn thing into motion.

At the front desk, a buck-toothed girl in a Holiday Inn-green jacket smiles real big at me as I stride with my newfound F.B.I. authority through the linoleum and fake wood paneled lobby. Behind her, through an open fake wood grain door, I see Brunhilde of the switchboard making sure no calls go in or out without her consent and indignation. She looks sort of like I'd pictured her: stout—jowly, in fact—bleached blonde beehive, too much arch on her pencilled-in eyebrows making her look surprised. All of this is pure Nevada style, but she's wearing fire engine red lipstick instead of the hot pink I anticipated. Yeech . . . She *is* reading a Harlequin romance! I want to . . . I feel like going over and . . . But I don't because I won't stoop to her level when there isn't time to do an effective job of it. Besides there's no one else in the lobby but the three of us and I like a bigger audience.

I pass through the first set of double doors into the nowhere zone set up between the cozy place for which travelers will fork over forty bucks a night and the hostile desert outside. I check up and down the length of the parking lot, cussing myself for freaking out over my car's paint job rather than with noticing how many or what kind of cars were parked out there when I arrived. And then there's the lot on the other side of the building that I didn't cruise through at all. Wish I had known how important gathering such information might be at the time.

This is a taste of my own medicine. None of the people I've tracked in my life for fun or profit or practice had or has ever guessed I was around. None to this day that I know of. Once we became Recovery Specialists, I was just the too-short cocktail waitress in sequins and a push-up bra full of cotton who stuck real close to the slot manager's station. Or the white-vinyl go-go booted blonde from the City feeding nickels into a machine while facing the craps tables. Or the new girl in the cashier's cage with horn-rimmed glasses and no access to anything except her cash drawer which happened to be right next to the counting room. It was fun for a while. Bread and butter. Fairly clean work, too. No busted-up marriages or seedy love trysts to photograph. Casinos are all about money, so generally no one gets hurt. Someone else's love in bed with someone else's sex is a different matter altogether—someone's always going to get hurt.

Now that I've been on the receiving end of a tail, I'll tell you I don't like it much. I've had to look over my shoulder before, but that was for truant officers and social workers or the Desert Diamond's goon squad who was trying to get us before we got them. Learning to outsmart government types was too, too easy and knowing from experience how to get around the trickier casino types has contributed greatly to my success as a snoop.

Then Mike comes along – a man over the line a lot farther than I am. Too many things tell me Mike's work had plenty of strings attached. Somebody out there's going to mind that Mike is dead. Or maybe somebody out there decided Mike was no longer useful. Could be he got greedy. I've seen that happen. Any way you look at it, it comes down to Flack keeping closer tabs on her ass. Best to assume that the unknown is unfriendly.

I cross the parking lot, tuned into everything around me but trying not to act completely casual. Smoking a cig. I climb into the hot interior of the GTO, put my key the ignition, and rev the engine. I put in the clutch and step on the brake to keep from rolling into the cement wall while I shift into reverse. I'm just about to back up when a black Mercedes comes fast from the east side of the Holiday Inn and jerks to a stop across my path just a few feet away from my rear bumper. The front passenger door flies open and a tall, skinny black dude with a huge 'fro, a fringed leather vest, and striped bell bottoms takes about a step and a half over to me before I have a chance to roll up the window and lock the door. He leans down putting his face close to mine. He's chewing a toothpick and wearing mirrored sunglasses. A bad imitation of Link from *Mod Squad*? But I ain't laughing.

"You wanna cut the engine?" he asks, taking the toothpick out of his mouth.

I don't want to but I turn off the motor.

"Something wrong?" I ask.

"Could be. You wanna step out the car?"

I don't want to but I step out, leaving my shoulder bag on the seat. "Link" holds my upper arm as he reaches clear across to grab my bag. He puts the strap over his shoulder. The leather and fringe match his vest exactly.

"Nice look on you," I say. He just switches the toothpick to the other side of his mouth and pats me down right there in the parking lot.

"Thanks, I guess," I say as he finishes running his hands up the insides of my thighs and starts rummaging in my bag. He comes up with the Python.

"Nice piece," he says, tucking the barrel down the front of his pants. If I ever get my gun back, I'll be washing that baby down with Lysol. Link leads me by the arm over to the Mercedes. The back windows are dark-tinted so you can't see inside. He opens the rear passenger side door, shoves me inside. Folds himself into the front seat and we take off: Link, me; at the wheel a white guy with two blond braids hanging over his shoulders and wearing a purple Hawaiian shirt, and beside me . . .

"Mona."

With a little mocha-tone baby, wrapped in a blankie with pink sheep on it, asleep against her deep, snowy neckline.

Weird.

I don't like weird.

Chapter 8

Mona and I go back a ways — a long ways. Back to when she was Sheryl and I was Susan Anne and my folks were still alive. Sheryl/Mona lived next door.

My Pop was a fireman; Sheryl's was a 21 dealer. And a coke head, like a lot of them. Sheryl's mom, her step-mother, really her second one — was the peach of a woman who eventually coached my mother in perfecting the kind of drinking and pill-popping that would kill her. The drinking those two did caused a big falling-out between me and Sheryl — well, Mona; hell, let's just go with Mona — because Mona herself apparently was born with a taste for drinking and the tolerance of an Irish coal miner. Or maybe the real attraction was that booze was the first thing she practiced stealing. Whichever came first, she had the bad taste to try to convince me that drowning my sorrows would be the healthiest way to deal with my Pop's death. Like I couldn't see the "positive" effects it was having on my own mother's grief. My friendship with liquor would come later.

Mona changed her name because that second step-mother's name was Cheryl too, but with a "C." Don't know why I never asked her how she settled on the name "Mona." But I hated that step-mother of hers almost as much as she did.

Changing her name to Ralph would have made as much sense. Seems strange that she tried to get some distance by adopting a new name and at the same time proceeded to do the very things to make herself become like the person she hated.

As if my mom wasn't losing it fast enough after Pop was killed, Mona's step-mother grabbed the golden opportunity to gain a drinking buddy. With Mona's dad always looking to get wired, he wasn't the best companion for the step-mom because her goal in life was to become immobilized. Luckily, at least the way she saw it, right next door was a friend indeed: a grieving widow, most of the way to catatonia on the natch. Conveniently located and highly suggestible. The two of them would start in drinking, usually at our house about ten a.m., and only quit when one or the other could no longer lift her glass. Mom generally outlasted Mona's step-mother through sheer willingness to get dead quick. Dose after recommended dose of Gilbey's vodka and Librium disappeared down their throats. Within six months, my mother fed her broken heart enough medicine to stop it. As far as I know, Mona's step-mom is still going strong. Remarried. Twice, last time I counted.

Mona used to swipe every misplaced bottle of Gilbey's she found. Kept shoving them in my face, especially after Pop's accident. She thought her step-mother and my mom were such a scream when they got all lit up, she wanted to get that way, too. And wanted a drinking buddy same as her step-mom did. I tried it a couple of times before things around my house got really complicated. With Mom always loaded and Timmy a handful of a twelve-year-old, I just didn't have the time to be screwing around. Had to keep something that resembled a household going. Mona and I argued the pros and cons of vodka-as-healer until finally, fighting with her was too much like work. I ended up having to push Mona out of my life – and not too gently. I could have used a friend back then, just couldn't use one with a bottle in her hand.

It wasn't until I put Timmy in prison that I took up a steady relationship with Jim Beam. Once upon a time, I had people besides just me to worry about. They kept me plenty busy. Later, when it was just me, I decided what the heck. Anyway, haven't you heard? I am indestructible. Knew it practically from birth. Why else am I the one left standing while everything around me goes perpetually to hell? When I was a kid, I thought if I concentrated—worried—hard enough I could keep bad things from happening. That idea didn't last long. Time and circumstances will always show you how silly you can be. I learned never to ask "what's next?" What's next gets here soon enough.

After Mom died and Timmy and I went to live with Red and Edie Larson and their six kids, I lost track of Mona for a good many years. There are just some people, though, that you're destined to spend your life crossing paths with. And every time I run across Mona now, she's into something new. Generally some sort of con. Sometimes dope. But from time to time she surprises me and pulls her talents into the straight-and-narrow long enough to make legit money in real estate or stocks or soybean futures. She has a good mind for that sort of thing. One of those people teachers said would have a bright future "if she'd only apply herself." She does "apply herself." Reads like a fiend. Taught herself to speak French with those Berlitz records. Refined herself. Had quit the booze cold the last time I saw her.

Somehow she picked up the manners of Jackie Kennedy and almost the speech except deeper, not as whispery. Not bad for a Reno girl from the crap end of Keystone Avenue. Basically, Mona's a criminal at heart. A restless one and thorough. Not stupid or emotional like my baby brother. I've never come close to putting a case together to catch Mona at her craft. I've tried. I mean, crime's crime no matter how close it is in your family. You'd think I'd have a different philosophy after what I did to Timmy, but I'd take Mona down in a second just to get her away from the bad guys. Whenever I start to get close, she goes underground. Off on some new venture before the old one gets cold. And in a few months or years, she jumps into my life again just to brag about what she's gotten away with and to tempt me with a few hints about her new direction. She loves that, as she says, "We share an intellect at crossed purposes." Yep, she talks like that. Honest. I hate for her to compare herself to me, but I also can't help being intrigued by the moves she makes, the way she thinks. I hate to hate what she does and admire how she does it simultaneously. If we were chess players, she'd be my favorite opponent.

So here we are on a Thursday afternoon in the back of someone's—she's not stupid enough to "invest" in cars—spanking-new Mercedes, shielded from public view by blackened windows, enjoying second-hand pot smoke from the guys up front. And we're tooling along nice and gradual in the completely opposite direction of both my office and my six o'clock appointment at Landrums.

"How are you, Flack?" Mona's leaning her lovely blonde head on the back of the seat, eyes closed, looks the picture of maternal contentment.

"Good, good. You?"

"Very well."

"Looks like you've been busy since I saw you last."

"Yes, her name is Pioche. Pioche Antoinette Lacroix."

Perfectly accented French. Anyway, sounded right to me.

"That's a mouthful. Why not Crawford? Change your last name, too?"

"Ever hear of women's lib? I *was* married. Briefly. Kept my name, though. Lacroix had a better ring to it than Crawford for Pioche."

"Congratulations."

78

"Thank you. It was delicious while it lasted. Superb for my French. And then there's . . ." She plays with the soft, dark curls on the baby's head and kisses her.

"Well, good buddy, what brings you to the Holiday Inn?"

Mona finally turns her perfectly coiffed, blonde head to look at me with sultry blue eyes and plenty of fake eyelashes. "Susan Anne, when will you do something with that hair? Aren't you rather mature for the Little Orphan Annie look?"

I try to squish down the volume of red curls. "Can't do a thing with it."

"I can recommend a marvelous salon on Arlington. Bruce will have you straightened out in no time."

"Pass. Sitting there for hours, smelling that goop, and listening to a bunch of pretentious small talk? Thanks but no thanks."

"Too bad. An up-and-coming businesswoman like yourself cannot afford not to look her very best."

The baby stirs and flexes her long fingers. I gesture toward the front seat. "Is Link there her father?"

"Rodney? Oh, heavens no. I know where her father is, but I don't care. She is lovely, is she not?"

Yes, she's beautiful. Wide forehead, pouty baby lips, long eyelashes.

"She's going to have hair as wild as mine, Mo," I say.

"Probably. We'll deal with that when the time comes."

We're headed west in no great hurry on picturesque Fourth Street. Past lumber yards, junk yards, every kind of automotive and hardware business. And also the only art supply store in northern Nevada. All old businesses looking older all the time. A few with what used to be nice neon signs that sputter even in the day but mostly storefronts with broken display windows and greasy sidewalks. People's perception of Reno is of the glitz downtown which is only three blocks wide and maybe six blocks long. The rest of our fair city's pretty pitiful with not enough exceptions to count.

"Ahem, as I was saying," changing the subject, "what brings you to the Holiday Inn?"

"Michael. Michael Parker. The word is he paid you an impromptu visit.

"Yeah, I think I remember him."

"You think you remember him."

"A lot of people pay me visits."

"Come now, you've only had the new place three months."

"Read about it in the business section, did you?"

"I endeavor to keep up."

"Why, thank you. What about Parker?"

"What did he want?"

"What do you think he wanted?"

Mona leans her head back again and closes her eyes.

"Flack, I find your little Sam Spade-envy routine quite irritating. Answering every question with a question, all that ridiculous cat and mouse."

"Hey, it's not like you just called me up and invited me over for tea. You kidnapped me out of a parking lot, remember? Your helper Rodney there felt me up good – not that I didn't appreciate the quality of his work – and relieved me of my gun. You haven't told me where we're going or why all the hassle or even if you like my shirt. The way I see it, you're the one owing me explanations."

Rodney turns toward us and offers me then Mona the joint. We both refuse. He says, "'s cool," and passes it to the driver.

"Rodney," Mona says, shifting the sagging weight of her baby into a more stretched out position, "what is Ms. Murrow carrying around in that hideous shoulder bag of hers?"

He pulls out my folded-up, yellow To Do list first. "It say here, 'Check Room 312. Call LaPetite 555-9876. Call 555-1764. Pick up item. Mail wallets.' First three things is crossed out. Don't say nothing else on there."

She faces me again. "'Item?' What is the item?"

"It's this . . . how do I describe it?" Especially because I have nothing in mind to create a suitable lie from. I go with my first thought something I know will bore Mona to tears and she'll beg me to shut up. "It's sort of a holder for a fishing pole. Spring loaded contraption that automatically set the hook if you get a bite. For lake fishing on the shore. Heard about it from a guy named Smitty I ran into out at Pyramid. He says . . ."

"Stop. I'm sure that's more than I wanted to know. What else is in there, Rodney?"

"She got a wallet, lipstick, smokes, Clorets, hairbrush, wallet . . ."

"You already said wallet," Mona says.

Rodney's quiet. Easy to stump a stoner. He fumbles around a little then he says, "They's two, Mona. Two wallets."

"Let me see them."

He holds them over the seat to her. She hands the sleeping Pioche to me. The baby dangles in front of me where I hold her under the arms. Kid keeps right on sleeping.

"Susan Anne, she's not a snake. Hold her."

I put the baby against me like Mona'd had her. Pioche's warm body settles against mine, and she appears not to mind the change of location from ample to bony. She grips my shirt sleeve in her brown fingers.

Mona goes through my wallet first. Nothing interests her except an old picture of Pop. She smiles, remembering him. Her family was so screwed up in all its incarnations, my Pop was the father she looked up to. We handled losing him in different ways: drowning in booze or keeping too busy to think, but I know she loved him. I see that in her face now: how much she misses the only person she ever allowed herself to give in and love. Until this baby, I hope. I hope Pioche means something to her. She hands my wallet back to Rodney, and opens Mike's.

"Hello Michael," she says.

"Oh, *that* Mike Parker."

"How did you come into possession of this article?"

The baby whimpers in her sleep. Just a little one. "He dropped it on his way out. Hole in the pocket of his overcoat, I guess."

"What did you two talk about that I'm sure you remember?"

"You know, the usual. The weather. Who has the best Friday night seafood buffet."

"That's what he came to discuss with you?"

"Look, Mo, he didn't get a chance to say much. He was falling-down drunk and running from something or someone. Two guys showed up and escorted him out."

"I see. Have you spoken with him since?"

"That wouldn't be too easy."

"In what way?"

"Let's just say he decided to change time zones."

"All right. You haven't seen him again?"

"Correct. Okay, we've established that I did make the acquaintance of Mike Parker. Now you owe me one. Where're we going?"

We're driving along the north bank of the Truckee River now where Fourth Street becomes Highway 40, passing trailer parks and the sleazy little motels with names like The Riffles and Sierra Pines. Most of the motels are little settlements of bungalows arranged around a horseshoe drive for easy in and out. They're also infamous for being the kinds of places you can rent by the hour. I've always thought the drive out Highway 40 along the Truckee was one of the most scenic roads around. When I was a kid, before Interstate 80 came through, this was *the* road to California. I remember it looking a lot more resort-y back then. Brunhilde's definition of a family place. Now with all of the traffic routed onto the

Interstate, the motels that haven't closed are infested with squatters and the trailer parks are filled with dented, pastel colored travel trailers whose wheels have rotted out from under them. I always feel like this beautiful place where the pines start deserves better than this.

Mona says, "Someone wants to see you."

"Who?"

"I believe that's 'whom.'" Let's just say he's the reason I asked Rodney to relieve you of your weapon."

"You work for this guy?"

"In a way."

"What way?"

"Personal services."

"I remember hearing somewhere that Mike worked for a guy in 'personal services,' too."

"There's a lot of that going around these days, I suppose. Susan Anne, what did Michael want?"

"You after anything specific here?"

Mona reaches over and takes the baby from me, kisses Pioche's pretty black curls. "Anything you might think should tell me you probably should before we reach to our destination."

"That would mean before we go see the person you're taking me to see?"

"Yes. Yes, that's precisely it."

"Does this person know what Michael wanted with me?"

"No, not fully. If you'll tell me now, I may be able to cover for you."

"I'll take my chances."

She leans down as if to pick up something from the seat between us and looks up at me. She keeps her voice low to keep the men in the front seat from overhearing.

"I need to talk to you. After. Soon."

I nodded and she straightens up.

We turn left onto a one-lane, dirt road leading to a narrow plank bridge crossing the Truckee. Rodney gets out to de-padlock a heavy chain blocking the access to the bridge. We drive over; he locks up and gets back into the car on the other side. It's just after three p.m., and the canyon we're headed into is already being cut up by long shadows. The road's surprisingly good for dirt. Out here, rocks crop up like dandelions and every drop of rain turns into a new gully. Usually the roads are like the surface of the moon. This one's been getting some daily TLC.

I say, "I don't much like going into iffy situations without my little six-shooting friend. You know what I mean, Mo?"

"Yes, I can sympathize. However, you are with me. Present company will keep you safe from harm. You have my word on that."

"Goody. Do I know this character? This guy I'm going to see? What's the dude's name?"

"Johnny. And you'll know him well enough soon enough."

"Okay, but I got an appointment at six for an earwax removal. Think you can get me out of here on time?"

Pioche stirs and opens her eyes as we come around a sharp turn. She looks at me cross-eyed, her mouth shaped like an "o," then bobs her head back and looks up at her mother. Mona makes a smiley Mom-face at the baby. Pioche yawns which makes her shiver all over. Their eyes lock onto each other's; they are the only two people in the world. Mona's face is soft and radiant. She's beautiful and simple, unmasked for a split second by love for her baby girl. I see Mona as she was when we were real little kids. Before life got its dirty paws on our security blankets.

"She's a cool baby, Mona. You're real lucky."

Mona kisses Pioche all over her face. The baby coos. "She's changed things for me, Susan Anne. Everything." I don't quite get the meaning in the look she gives me but there's a lot mixed up in it. I shrug, "so?" She shakes her head to indicate that we're not going to talk about this right now.

"Johnny, huh? What line of work is he in?"

"Everything he wants."

"Jack-of-all-trades?"

"More of an investor," she says as she pokes a finger under the elastic legband of Pioche's plastic pants and inspects the condition of the diaper. "A man of means."

And she flashes me that look again.

Chapter 9

Deeper into the canyon, sagebrush gives up some ground to junipers and piñons which give up a little bit more to a few scattered pine trees. Scrawny Nevada pines. Or by now we could be in the early stages of California. You can live in Reno all your life and still be amazed how close you are to the state line. The pines we're passing are spindly and far apart, but the hills are so close together, we're winding through a deep ditch of shadow. Except that I know we're headed west along the Truckee, I'm not sure exactly where we are.

Pioche woke up happy, and she's keeping us entertained, laughing at Mona's way-out-of-character funny faces. The baby's an expert drooler. A long thread that will reproduce itself instantly if wiped off hangs from her bottom lip and connects to her little pink dress at belly-level. Just now, Mona looks like she truly might make it as the kind of settled-down mom she claims to want to be. If she brings the devotion she's demonstrated in finding ways to separate her unsuspecting victims from their money into her child rearing, I don't think she can miss raising a kid with her head screwed on securely.

For all cool the places she's been, she can't seem to stay away from Reno-Tahoe. With her style and brains, she could be a power in a place like LA or Miami or New York City. I, on the other hand, know what keeps me here: room to move. And assorted memories. Here, in no more than ten minutes in almost any direction, you can set foot on millions of acres of empty desert with only a few small towns to mess with and those being miles and miles apart. Lovelock, Ely, Tonopah, Pioche, Mona's baby's namesake village way out east. Some of the towns that still show up on the map are dead or nearly dead and don't take up much space: Beowawe, Goldfield, Austin. Then there's Vegas—yeah, you have to mention it—but that's a planet from another galaxy I personally wish we didn't need to mention.

I know I'll never leave Nevada. Why should I? For all the heartache I've known in my life here, I love living in the last of the wild, wild West. Dirty enough to be fun, clean enough to, well, be able to breathe. I want a never-closes lifestyle. I want to walk into Ben's at 4 am and buy some Beam. Then scoot over to the Cal-Neva for 99¢ ham and eggs. I love hearing those coins falling out of slot machines into the hands of winners. I love the smell of stale cigarette smoke and spilled booze. I love the smell of pinon pine burning in the campfire. I love eating the pitchy nuts those scraggly trees produce even if it's a sticky-icky job to collect them. I love the Nevada Day parade in Carson City, which happens to take place on Halloween, and Carson kids trick-or-treat the day before. October 31, 1864, was our admission day. The Yankees needed Nevada's silver to help finance the Civil War and its votes to wipe out the Confederacy. Whether Nevadans know their history or not—and, dammit, they should — people get drunker than $700 as my father used to say (and I still don't know what it means) out on Carson Street watching the parade, then put the kids in the care of some remaining less-drunk soul, and adjourn to Jack's Bar or the Old Globe and keep right on going. The annual beard contest is a highlight generally dominated by the esteemed members of E Clampus

Vitus, who are also in charge of poop scooping behind the parade horses so the bands and the majorettes and the tumbling teams don't have to walk through slimy, green manure. The Clampers in their red union suit long-johns, beatup hats, suspenders, overalls, and epic beards are scraggly and rough and 100% Nevada. Don't know what the parade or the Virginia City camel races would do without them. Drunk Clampers riding camels and ostriches down the Comstock main drag are a sight to see. Brings tears to my eyes just thinking about that festive day in September. Where else in America are you going to see that?

What else could I want? I have mountains, Lake Tahoe and Pyramid, the Truckee River, lots of open range to ride, rabbits and cans to plink at, not many rules. And not many people. In 1973 the whole state has only a half a million in 110,000 square miles. A little birdie (thanks, Mo) told me New York City has, like, 16 million in 300 square miles. 16 MILLION? Eeeewwwww! If I had my way, there wouldn't even be that half a million here.

I'm Reno, born and raised, Nevada Battle Born, even though lot has changed since I was a kid, almost all of it not for the better. Those houses made of ticky-tacky that I fucking hate? Sprouting like some kind of measles on the outskirts of town. They're widening 395 and 80 to handle more and more cars. There are new casinos popping up. The hotels are getting taller and uglier, but Jessie Beck's and the Mapes are still going strong, thank gawd. One of the first. Frank Sinatra, Liberace, and Judy Garland have always been headliners in Reno. That's something. The glamorous El Cortez Hotel is disintegrating into a flophouse. Danny Thomas used to stay there when he was in town. So did Carol Channing.

The good part of our progress? We have three t.v. stations now: 2, 4, and 8, but I hear we're going to get cable. Pretty soon we'll be bombarded with California crap. I hear KTVU-2 from Oakland is pretty good, though.

Star route addresses, party lines, and volunteer fire departments are fading away. More and more parts of our lives are getting taken out of our hands by government and big companies. That kind of "progress" I do not love.

I do completely, forever, without a doubt love the desert. I do love the desert. The aloneness. The hard life. No fences, no funky green grass parks or "official" hiking trails. The straightforward elegance of bare hills and sagebrush is as beautiful to me as a diamond solitaire. Lucky for us sand-lubbers that most people can't see what we see in the desert, and we have it all to ourselves. Just us and a few harmless or damn harmful critters. I keep promising myself that if I go on living much longer, I'll chuck it all and become a model desert rat: a wild-haired recluse with a fifty-gallon water tank on the back of a beat-up flatbed that I'll reluctantly drive into town to fill now and then. Wouldn't bother me a bit to see civilization for no other reason than that.

Mona, on the other hand, needs people. Not that she likes them any better than I do. It's how she operates. I can't imagine her not taking something from someone by the most sneaky of means. She thrives on plots. And you need suckers for that. I'd think she'd want more of them than she can come in contact with in Nevada. But she keeps coming back and seems to find enough of them here to keep her satisfied. Briefly.

The whole state is one big shell game: everybody trying to get someone else's . . . You fill in the blank. Usually it's money, but even when the game's about love, you can bet money's not too damn far under the surface. Being able to play both money and love to her own ends makes Mona a big fish in this small pond, and maybe that's as hard as she wants to work. She knows this game perfectly. All she's had to do is put to use her early childhood education provided by the weak, backhanded adults who raised her. She knows just what number to dial to take a person's psyche apart.

She's not wholesome. I'm not wholesome. Nevadans over all don't mess around pretending we want such an image, no matter what our politicians claim. We're happy to lure people from Portland and Sacramento and, God forbid, Salt Lake City to come here and have the high old times they'd die of embarrassment if the people back in their squeaky-clean hometowns knew about. If you're here, you've agreed to the game. Maybe that's why I stay, and maybe that's why Mona keeps Nevada on her list: things are raw but they're right in front of you. Right where you can keep an eye on them. And make a quick buck.

"Are we there yet?" I say.

Mona located a baby bottle full of milk in a pink striped baby bag on the floor of the car. She's cradling Pioche, feeding her, talking to her.

"Patience, child," Mona says to me without looking over.

"Just helping you get used to hearing it. And I didn't go to the bathroom before we left either."

"Here's your chance. We've arrived."

We reach the top of a steep rise in the road and whoa Nelly! Stark white plaster, black trim and iron beams. Miles of glass. About six thousand square feet of expensive building materials arranged in the goofiest way to make a house. Looks like a sci fi movie set. A little *2001* plopped down on a clearing in the drab high desert. We pull in under a galvanized metal roof held up by black girders strung together with industrial strength cables and turnbuckles and big bolts — all painted black.

I can't help it. I say, "Note the way the architecture utilizes the natural surroundings to create a home that seems to have grown organically from the soil upon which it rests." I watch too much PBS.

"Like it?" says Mona as she gathers up Pioche's stuff.

"Cozy."

As soon as we stop, the pig-tailed driver gets out of the car, slams the door, and walks directly away to a smaller, though similarly designed building. Opens the door, goes inside, slams the door without looking back. How can a person be that cranky while stoned on pot?

Rodney gets out, opens my door then saunters around behind the car to get Mona's. He hands her my gun. She hands him the baby and the bottle before getting out with both of her arms full of pink and white items and my leather shoulder bag. Rodney croons to the baby as we follow them to a pair of purple doors, both of which he pushes wide open for us. Inside is a sterile, white space with a gleaming white tile floor and a high, flat black ceiling. The wiring and duct work up there are exposed and running every direction. Rodney disappears down a hallway, talking jive to Pioche.

"Guess this Johnny guy couldn't afford to finish the place, huh?" I say, inspecting the ceiling.

"Doubtful. I'm sure some charlatan sold him on the idea of 'making a statement.' He's a gifted businessman but a sucker for experts in any field of art. You'll see more evidence of that in the living room. If you were serious about finding a powder room, there is one to your left. Second door."

"Thanks. Don't mind if I do."

The powder room is painted fresh-blood red and is the size of most kitchens. Black and white striped floor. Shiny black fixtures. Chrome everywhere chrome could possibly be. A Jacuzzi spa tub. A urinal — black. Quaint. A black wall-mounted telephone beside the john. The color scheme of this whole place is getting monotonous. Through the floor-to-ceiling, wall-to-wall window behind the tub, the natural world looks like a dollar bill that's gone through the washer too many times. Just not enough oomph out there to compete with this super-charged decor.

I pee and tidy up. Push my hair into a more compact shape. Try to shake off some of the effects of the day. I slap on a new game face for whatever kind of dog and pony show I'll be expected to perform next. When I come out, Mona's still waiting in the entry.

"Don't let him make you crazy," she whispers. And she looks serious.

The evidence of Johnny's infatuation with, but lack of taste in, art explodes when you enter the living room. It's packed with arty goo-gaws — hanging, standing, in motion. Most of it looks like it came out of the electric sign junkyard on Vassar. Sort of half done or half thrown away. But colorful. A relief from all the white. Johnny is seated, or rather cradled, amid the chaos in a huge — you guessed it, black — leather armchair. He's got the white Topsiders and no socks. White polyester bellbottoms. A shiny red shirt — on but unbuttoned. I'd put his age at about twenty-two, twenty-three. Handsome as hell. Looks like the Mexican my two jailbirds described to me. I might have known.

"Ladies," he says without getting up but opening his hands slightly in a gesture of royalty welcoming the peasants. "Here you are."

Mona goes over to him and they hold one kiss for a long time. Personal services, apparently. When she comes up for air, she introduces me.

"Johnny, this is Susan Anne, pardon me, Flack Murrow."

"When I first heard of you, I thought you'd be a guy. Yeah," he says. He runs the index fingers of both hands behind his ears to smooth back his long hair.

"Happens to me a lot," I say.

"Yeah, I guess it would in your gig. You ladies want a drink? Help yourselves." He flips another pretty hand gesture at the bar to our right that you couldn't miss blindfolded.

Under about a billion watts of heat from rows and rows of sparkly glass bulbs over the chrome bar, I pour my usual. Mona has a tall tonic and ice. We sit at one end of a very long black leather couch, close but not too close to Johnny. I'm taking my cues from Mona, but I do wonder about her appetite for men. I can hear people talking in some other part or parts of the house. Sounds like quite a few voices. Less than twenty but more than five. And coming from where?

"Well, here she is," Johnny says to Mona.

"Yes."

"Has she seen Michael?"

"Briefly. I thought you'd want to question her yourself."

"Yeah, for sure. So, did he blow it?" he asks her.

"Blow it?"

"You know, spill?"

"Hey, you guys," I say. "I don't mean to interrupt but I *am* in the room."

Mona puts her foot on top of mine. From the quick look she gives me I understand that you talk when Johnny says you can talk in his house. He's got his hands steepled under his chin, his foot bouncing with impatience where it's crossed over his knee. I settle back with my glass of bourbon and divide my attention between their conversation and the ones going on in other rooms that I find, no matter how hard I try, I cannot make out. Just the highs – laughs, little exclamations.

"Flack?"

Am I finally being addressed?

"Yes, Mona?"

"Michael, about whom we were speaking on our way here, is a friend of Johnny's. A business partner as well. Last night, he and Johnny had a . . . disagreement. Michael disappeared. It was I who traced him to you. Johnny is concerned about what you two may have had opportunity to discuss. Also, anything you might tell him regarding the whereabouts of Michael would significantly shorten the duration of your visit here."

I love the way she talks. Kind of like the directory assistance lady you call up at Ma Bell. Real slow and clear. Forming every letter of every word.

"Do I tell you or tell him?" I ask.

Johnny says, "Go ahead. Tell me."

"Okay, it's like this. He didn't say much because he was stinking drunk."

Johnny looks at Mona. She looks him straight in the eye— straighter than I've ever seen her look at anyone. Which makes me suspicious. This news appears to be both a relief and a nuisance to them. Neither one acts neutral about hearing it.

"Shall I go on?" I ask.

"Michael, he gets crazy sometimes. Yeah," Johnny says. Then he says, "Continue."

"Like I told Mona, before we could chat two charming gentlemen showed up and escorted him out. Don't know where and don't want to know where. But, Mikey was waiting for me in my office when I showed up this morning."

Johnny leans forward, hands on his knees. "And . . .?"

"He was kind of quiet. He was kind of dead."

Mona puts her hand over her mouth. Not all dramatic — just surprised. Johnny looks down at his hands. His skinny shoulder blades almost meet behind his neck. He slumps back into his nest of a chair, his delicate fingers extended on the overstuffed arms. He doesn't look so good.

Mona clears her throat. "Flack had his wallet in her bag when we picked her up." She gets up and takes the wallet to him. He opens it and thumbs through before slinging it across the room. Mona ducks, seeing movement out of the corner of her eye as the wallet sails by. It smacks into a standing goo-gaw with feathers coming out of what is probably its head, making it rock on its pedestal. Mona quickly sits back down by me and flashes me a signal with her eyes. A warning.

Johnny's out of his chair and sitting on the glass coffee table in front of me as fast as I've ever seen anyone move. He spreads my knees apart with his hands, positions himself between them, and scoots in closer to me. His knees touch the insides of my thighs. I hate to admit it but now that I see him up close, he's one of those doe-eyed bad guys we ladies will fall all over ourselves to be misused by. He may be skinny and short, but he's long on that new guy's—what's his name? yeah, Al Pacino's—intensity I can feel all over.

"Did you take anything else from Michael? If you did, I want it." His smooth face is inches from mine.

"Mr. uh, Johnny – you mind if I call you Johnny? – I didn't *take* shit. I told you he dropped the damn wallet."

Johnny leans forward and puts his hands on my legs. Leans on them. Looks me in the eye, smiling.

"You know he was following you? Yeah, a couple of months. Since before you got the new place."

"Is that right? What for?"

"I told him to."

Some days that start out creepy just get creepier.

"You were having me followed?" Which at least clears up the reason for Michael's notebook. A job, not a stalking. I glance over at Mona whose eyes reveal nothing.

"Uh huh."

"You think he got all smitten with me and decided to tattle on you?"

"Dig this chick," he says to Mona. Then he focuses his attention back on me. "What did he tell you?"

"About what?"

"Goddam, you always answer a question with a question?"

"Why not?"

He starts rubbing his hands up and down the tops of my legs. The pressure's building. He's thinking. He wants a statement, I'll give him a statement.

"You're going to tell me why you were having me followed. You're going to tell me now."

Muscles of disbelief scrunch up his eyes and turn his lips into a straight line. "Nope," is all he manages to get out.

"Nope?" I say. I take hold of his hands and remove them snippily from my legs. I feel the movement of Mona hustling out of the way just before our friend Johnny lets me have it on the side of my face with the flat of his hand.

"Johnny!" I hear Mona scream. It wasn't that hard a slap, but it did get my attention and make my ear ring a little. I figure tit for tat, so smiling as cheerily I can, I return the favor and smack the victory sneer off Johnny's handsome face.

"Susan Anne!"

While he's getting over the shock, I roll off the back of the couch and pick up a long, metal art-cha-dingy from the narrow table behind me to use as a weapon. Mona was right to disarm me. This man gets on your last nerve fast.

"Come on, bitch," he yells. "You want some of this?" Switchblade. Figures. He tosses the knife from hand to hand like he's trying out for a high school production of *West Side Story*.

"Nah," I say. "I think I'll take my frustrations out on this." I swing the art-cha-dingy from right to left and cut the thing with the feathers coming out of its head in half.

"Man, that cost me four grand!"

"You were robbed." I swing my weapon again, straight down and chop into the back of the couch. Down to the wooden frame. The edge gets momentarily stuck in the wood, but I pull it free and swing it back into an attack position. This thing's handier—and a whole lot sharper and heavier—than I thought. Johnny's dancing from side to side, trying to get me to flinch the wrong way. I take aim at a blown glass vase—probably one of the least tasteless objects in the room. It'd be a shame to . . .

"Stop, you two. Now!" Mona's got my .357 gripped in steady, practiced hands, leveling it first at Johnny and then at me. All kinds of cool.

"Well, he started it," I say.

Johnny thrusts his blade at me. I'm ready to heave the whatchamacallit at him, even though it's becoming a struggle to keep it raised with both hands. We must look like we're in a cartoon sword fight.

"You want to end it? Come on," he says.

My arms are tired now. And since, after all, Mona does have a gun and she is an old friend, I physically declare a draw: go and sit in my old place on the couch, the whatchadingy across my lap, and slug down the rest of my drink. I'd light a cigarette, but Johnny might mistake the shaking of my exhausted arms for fear. Can't let him know I'm anything but in charge, calm and collected. Mona settles on the arm of Johnny's chair and kisses the top of his head as he sits down. He unswitches the switchblade, slides it into his left front pants pocket. Mona holds the Python pointed at the floor by her side away from him.

"Now, can we behave like adults?" I ask.

You can tell I've stretched Johnny's patience as far as it can go. Mona massages his near shoulder and says in her phone company voice, "Let her speak, Johnny."

He waves "go ahead." Steeples his hands under his chin again.

"Your friend did a real pro's job of tailing me, it's true. Couldn't have done better myself and I'm damn good. Taught me a lesson: got to pay better attention in this business. I ought to thank you but . . . Now, since you already know everything about me, I want to know exactly what the goddam hell is going on with you people."

"I can answer that," Mona says. She glances at Johnny. "That is if you don't mind, honey."

"Shoot. It was your idea."

"Johnny needed some professional assistance. I recommended you. But he had misgivings when I told him you're a woman."

"I have misgivings about that myself sometimes." Mona looks perturbed at me. "Just kidding. Keep going."

"Johnny asked Michael to keep tabs on you for a while. Watch you work."

"Mikey did slightly more than that. He even wrote down who I slept with. Or is that part of this 'assistance' you expected from me?"

"Oh, don't you wish . . ." Johnny says before Mona shuts him down with a hand on his arm.

"Now . . ." Mona doesn't finish her sentence. Then she says, "Everything's changed."

"Gee," I say. "I'm fired? What a day! I get to work, there's a stiff in my chair, I get kidnapped out of the Holiday Inn, and then I get fired from a job I never started. Can you beat that?"

Johnny rubs that spot above the bridge of his nose that aches on all of us when we're tense and says, "You're set pretty fine, Flack." He emphasizes the "k" in my name with enough venom to embarrass a rattlesnake. "You can make any move you want. Yeah. You got the goods on the cops, the fire department, casino bosses, security guards. You got no friends. No boyfriend. No enemies. If I didn't hate your fucking guts already, I'd put you on the permanent payroll this second."

"In your wildest dream," I say.

Johnny looks away from me out the windows for a long, silent moment. I can't decide if he's depressed or bored or tired. Finally he asks, "Tell me, how did Michael . . .?"

"Buy it? Armload of the good stuff. Veterinary works."

Johnny nods. Looks over at the windows again. Realizes something. Or is hoping he hasn't given something away. Mona's fidgeting like she knows more than she should, too.

"You kill him?" I ask Johnny.

He shakes his head without looking at me. He seems gloomy for a split second, I wonder if he thinks *I* killed him. I look at Mona. I don't ask the same question, but you never can tell with her. Somewhere in the house, rock music starts thumping. I hear people moving around, still talking.

"What gives in this house, Johnny?"

"Meaning?"

"You got a big family or big rats or what?"

"I take in strays." He runs his hands over his slick, black hair. "Listen, I could be generous to the person who finds out who killed Michael."

"I'll see what I can do."

"You'll see what you can do in twenty-four hours, babe."

"Done, dear."

All of this time Mona's watching me. It's our old look – the one we used to give each other as kids when the story we were telling or the trouble we were in was going to require collaboration and a bit of acting. She knows her part here; I'm playing along as much as I can. She's mixed me up in something uncool and strictly for her own, selfish convenience, and I'm damn ticked off at her right now. But this is not the time or place to bitch about it.

I say, "Well, groovy. I'll see what I can find out and get back to you tomorrow then, Same Bat-time, same Bat-channel." I check my watch. "Hey, Mo, can you get your driver to take me back into town? I'm going to be late for my appointment."

She looks at Johnny who I know will be leaving the house soon for his own appointment. He nods just once. Smooth.

"Tomorrow," Johnny says, pointing one of his pretty forefingers at me like the Uncle Sam "I Want You" poster. "I'll have someone pick you up at your office at six sharp. Tomorrow night," he says. "And don't disappoint me."

"Wouldn't think of it, you've been a damn hospitable host." I get up. As I pass by, I touch and admire the slash I made in Johnny's couch. Mona stands, puts the .357 into my bag, and gives the bag to me.

"Thanks."

"Don't try nothing funny. You know I got eyes," says Johnny.

"And handsome ones they are, too. Thanks for the drink."

"Mona, get her a ride."

"I'll be right back," Mona says, kissing him.

She and I head for the sterile white entryway. I still hear voices and music and, closer by, the gleeful squeal of Mona's baby, Rodney's talking.

"Gee, Mona, you guys are practically Ozzie and Harriet out here. All American family scene."

She pushes a button on the intercom. "Duke? Duke, are you over there?"

A metallic voice comes back. "What?"

"I need you to take my friend back to Reno. Right away."

I hear an irritated sigh. "Fine." He clicks off abruptly.

Mona turns to me and says in a low voice, "Be careful, Susan Anne."

"What have you got me tangled up in, Mo?"

"It didn't start out . . . I thought I had considered every angle. Damn it. Our conversation in there? It wasn't remotely close to the truth on Johnny's part nor on mine. You see, I told both he and Michael a pretty fairy tale about you knowing something they're not supposed to know you know, if that makes any sense."

I say, "Gee." What else is there to say?

"I'm sorry I got you into this," Mona says. "I had good reason but no right, and I swear I'll get you out. Then I'm done."

"Done with what?"

She spreads her arms out to the sterile palace. "Everything."

"Meaning . . .?"

"I intend to disappear. Take my baby. Join some PTA group in Kansas. You'll no doubt be happy never to hear from me again."

"Aw shucks, Mo. Are you breaking up with me? I've got to tell you, none of this sounds right. Who's Michael to you, anyway? And what's the deal with this Johnny? I see he's rich, but he doesn't strike me as much else, especially not as a main squeeze, no offense."

"You are very wrong there. He's extremely powerful. In many ways."

"Shows you looks can be deceiving."

"Susan Anne, he's . . ."

"Mona!" Johnny calls from his throne.

"I'm coming," she says with more than a hint of irritation or fear in her voice. She lowers her tone, "Pioche and I, we need your help now. Please?"

"Hey, what're friends for? Just don't expect me to do anything too crooked."

"No, no, I never would — you know that — or I would have tried it long ago." Mona opens one side of the purple front doors. "Watch yourself. Johnny's trouble. Too many brains, too much money, too much gut instinct and absolutely no control."

The same blond driver, Duke or Smiley, who brought us out here flips a cigarette away irritably as he marches across the newly-paved driveway to the car. He gets in, slams the Mercedes' door, settles himself behind the wheel, and guns the motor.

"You be careful, too, Mo. You got that baby to think about."

"Yes, yes, I know. We'll all be out of this soon."

That Mona. She's a real pistol.

It's 5:30.

Chapter 10

I open the car door myself and climb into the back seat of the Mercedes. Duke throws it into gear and takes off before I even get my feet all the way inside. I see Mona, standing in front of the purple doors with her arms crossed, watching me leave. Johnny comes up behind her, wraps his arms around her waist, slides one hand a little farther down and holds her by the crotch. She lays her head back against his shoulder. I can only hope she's pretending she likes this.

Smiley up front is driving out of the canyon like we're being chased by the Feds. Must need to dump me and get back home in time to catch John Firpo's mouth telling the evening news. No kidding: the rest of Firpo's face never moves. Just the lips and those just barely. Duke/Smiley would appreciate that.

Other than listening to the whine of the over-revved engine and having to grab onto the door handle to keep from falling over every now and then, I guess this will be a fairly quiet ride. My chauffeur doesn't seem to be much for talk of any size or kind. When I realize I haven't had a cigarette in hours and ask Mr. Congeniality if he minds if I light up, my request gets a dismissive wave of his right hand. I shake a Lucky out of the pack and note that he's blowing the air blue with pot smoke anyway.

As we're flying down the canyon faster than the dust on Johnny's private drive a mile behind us has a chance to settle, I roll the events of the past couple of days around in my mind to see how they taste. One from columns A, B, C and D. A lot to think about and I haven't had much time to do it. It was a drag to find out that after all was said and done, Mona and Johnny both had contributed nothing but equal parts of bullshit to our conversation. Good of her to let me in on that information just as I was leaving, though. None of what was said makes me any more sure about where to go from here with this Johnny thing. Other than to Landrums in—yikes, twenty minutes.

"Personal services." Strikes me all of a sudden that I've heard that phrase twice now, both times in the context of someone's association to Johnny. Seems to cover the gambit of occupations from keeping Johnny cuddly and warm to following a private investigator around to see how she behaves. Wonder what kinds of "personal services" the people I heard but never saw in his house provide for him. And I wonder, too, what sordid task he planned on hiring me to carry out. Or was that another part of Johnny and Mona's big untruth?

The guy's used to telling people what to do. He seems kind of young for that. Kind of young for the money it'd take to build the house I just came from regardless of how you feel about his taste. His edgy air of command, at any rate, is no put-on. Some've got it, most don't, and people catch on to the fakes pretty fast. I didn't detect an ounce of hesitation from him. Johnny seems to have no trouble feeling like people owe him what he demands. That's all it takes to lead: make the masses believe they *want* to do what you say. They'll do it without thinking nine and a half times out of ten. He leads, they follow, but down what primrose path?

And Johnny might think he is, but he is *not* leading Mona around by the nose. No. This girl is always out for herself. If she's putting up with any kind of personal service situation at Johnny's, it's because she benefits in some way. She's never willingly played second-fiddle to anyone and for her the only numbers that count would be One and Two. One is getting what you want and ending up where you want to be. Two is whoever might be catching up to grab it all away. Everyone else is just flesh taking up space.

I imagine there must be some hot times between the two of them, having popped out of pretty much the same mold. But *she's* working *him*. The way she works he can't tell that she's not interested in a man for sex or gratitude or love or protection like most women—"liberated" or not. At least, she's never let herself be distracted by such trivia in the past. For her to be putting on this act, Johnny's got to have something she wants bad. Something with a big dollar sign in front of it, otherwise I don't think she'd keep her baby in close confines with just some garden-variety, handsome, rich maniac – especially not one with as a short a fuse as Johnny's. From what little she hinted to me about wanting to get permanently out of the life she's been living, she must be onto an ultimate score.

◊

"Where you want me to drop you?" Smiley grumbles.

"Back at the Holiday Inn if you would please."

He lets out disgusted breath and squirms lower into his seat. We'd just crossed Keystone and had to stop at the light at Fourth and Vine by the Gold and Silver Club. They serve good spaghetti there. Plenty of meat in the sauce. Now that Highway 40 isn't a main route into town anymore, the Gold and Silver has become a locals' dive. I like it. The up-keep on the building itself is falling apart fast because good food and a quiet bar don't keep bills paid in the casino business, and locals don't pump nearly enough nickels into the machines. They'll come to shoot the breeze and eat cheap, but except for a few older women with too much time on their hands and who live right there in the neighborhood, locals rarely try their luck at the Gold and Silver. And now, with the Interstate, tourists almost never do.

Since we've barely gotten into the west side of town-proper, Duke's not the least bit happy that I'm making him take me east practically to Sparks. I look at my watch. Ten to six. No way Smiley's going to catch the news tonight. Bummer. And it dawns on me if I go to get my car now, I'll be late to witness the rendezvous between Johnny and my two jailbirds. Strange how you can fall into one thing – or have one thing, named Michael, fall on you – and practically every person or event in your life for the next little while will somehow relate to that thing that fell. Almost makes you believe in destiny, if figuring out life is your hang-up. To me, these are just interesting threads coming together. I'm nosy. I want to see where they all came from and where they'll go.

Johnny will come to collect his baseball cards—which I have safe and sound at home. Johnny'll be in a lousy mood when Heckle and Jeckle tell him they've failed on their mission to get his stuff back from Michael. They'll give him a song and dance about how they had to spend the night in jail. Tell him about the mouthy broad who sent them there overnight then showed up again to harass them this morning. They'll show him my card. And he'll flip out. But they'll also, if they follow my instructions, give him back the two hundred bucks he paid them since their mission was never accomplished. Hopefully, that will square things between the three of them and they can all go their merry ways in peace. And then there's me . . .

"Hey," I say to my friendly, courteous driver. "I changed my mind. How about dropping me at House of Lung Fung? I feel like some moo goo gai pan." Lung Fung's is across the street from Landrums. Sounds like a good vantage point. Plus I'm hungry.

"She waits til we're clear to Wells Avenue . . ." he grumbles. Then he circles back to Virginia Street. He should be thanking me: Lung Fung's is closer to where we are now than the Holiday Inn is. Means he can split sooner, back to the Ponderosa or the Brady Bunch or whatever the hell they have going out there at Johnny's. With the change in my itinerary, I can be on time to watch the evening's entertainment and enjoy a tasty meal besides.

Chapter 11

Lung, the proprietor of my favorite eatery, is one of those historical Reno-ites. A local fixture everyone waves to and recognizes a mile away. He's got this distinctive walk. Knees pumping out to the sides. Black pants — always black pants— swinging around his skinny legs as he goes. He also wears white short sleeve dress shirts, every day of the year. And is he quick! Getting someplace in a hurry. Usually the bank or the Nevada Club when he's not at his restaurant.

Anybody who's lived in Reno for any time at all has eaten at House of Lung Fung. More than once. As for tourists, Lung's is on the right street—the main drag—but too far from the action, so his restaurant draws a strictly local crowd. As much as he loves to gamble, you'd think he'd put in a few slots to pass the time and to lure in the odd, off-course out-of-towner. He must prefer to separate work and play. Poker's his favorite casino game anyway, and there's not a machine yet that's figured out how to play it. Wouldn't be any fun for Lung if such an item did exist. No eyes to look into.

Back before it was his place, Lung Fung's was briefly a coffee shop. Back when my Pop was a teeny-bopper. Why anyone would think to open an American food joint across from Landrums amazes me still. And I wasn't even alive when whoever it was – probably some smarter-than-thou Californian – got the bright idea to go into competition with the best gringo grub in northern Nevada.

Landrums is one of those forties prefab diners that you could buy out of a catalog and then plunk down on the site of your choice and, voila!, you're open for business. Green and white on the outside with a pink neon sign – just the one word "Landrums" in script. Inside, sheets of diamond-patterned chrome screwed to the walls. A green, fake marble counter with chrome trim. Six green vinyl-upholstered stools, worn smooth and dark from a history of butts sliding on and off. No tables.

What Landrums lacks in seating capacity, it makes up for on the menu. Locals for decades would rather lean against the sweaty windows and eat or wait outside on the bus bench for a spot to free up than to eat anywhere else. Best chili-cheese omelet on the planet. Always drips onto the counter. Precisely the right thing you can eat before going to bed when you've accidentally had way too much to drink. He-man coffee in scarred, tan cups. Mismatched silverware. Burgers with gobs of onions. The usual, only somehow better. Maybe just the aged quality of the grease.

But while we all know Lung and the history of his joint, there seems to be a general amnesia about the who of Landrums. No one can recall meeting anyone named Landrum. Ever. The place is open twenty-four hours a day, seven days a week yet there has never been a sighting of anyone coming to take the money to the bank or checking on supplies or saying howdy-do to the customers. One cook and one waitress who look strangely the same on every shift run the place and gripe about having to be there but never mention a boss. The place never changes; the menu never changes (except when the prices that get scratched out and rewritten in blue ink). The waitress and the cook never get younger or older. It's eerie if you take the time to notice these things. Most people don't; they just go for the food which never fails. And don't ask.

Eventually Lung gets hold of the coffee shop on the opposite corner from Landrums. Changes the menu over to Chinese. Nothing too exotic — fried rice and prawns and excellent moo goo gai pan. Puts up some red-on-red flocked wallpaper, those white Chinese lamps with painted landscapes and red tassels over the booths. Moved the cash register from the back by the kitchen to smack dab in front of the front door. No getting past Lung. And like Landrums, the decor has never changed. It just gets darker and darker from the greasy kind of flame-throwing cooking going on there.

You couldn't call Lung's a hot spot. Especially now. The place has kind of settled into itself like comfy slippers. Lung made his money. But other people need work, and he provides it. And I don't think he'd like it much if he couldn't yell at a cook or two on a daily basis. It's one of those places that's just *there*. Take it or leave it. Not a date place. Nothing to write home about.

A few of us—me included—love the place out of pure nostalgia. Once upon a time, because you could count on always getting a seat and having your order served in a hurry, Lung's became a hangout for the guys from the police and fire departments. The unofficial meeting place of the minds. The food was tasty and cheap and fast. The location was good. Lung and his crew never seemed to mind how loud the guys were or get all freaked out about a mob of them showing up at once. All of us still go there—the guys and their families and one by one, the families of their families. That's why I go, though most of them don't have much to say to me anymore. The new guys mostly hang out at their favorite MacDonalds or Taco Bell. No accounting for taste. For us old timers, House of Lung Fung is like an unofficial Elks lodge: we just keep going out of habit.

My Pop wasn't just another #4 with egg flower soup for long once he and Lung discovered they were members of the same holy order: lovers of the game of Hearts. Any time Pop showed up, Lung would drop everything and the two of them would play in the back booth Lung reserved for family for as long as they each could spare. Even when Mom and Timmy and I were with him for a family dinner, he and Lung would sneak off together to play a few hands. Lung bet lunches; Pop bet two bucks a game. Pop ended up paying for a lot of lunches. They were a sight: my Pop, a mountain of a man with huge hands and a booming voice; tiny Lung in a dirty white half-apron, short sleeve white dress shirt, horn-rimmed glasses sliding down his bridgeless nose. Bickering like two old ladies over their cards.

Lung's really old now. Pushing up thicker, heavier glasses. He isn't around the restaurant all the time anymore. Lets his daughter-in-law sit at the register. He likes to hang out at the Nevada Club, drinking free VO and waters, and playing poker or blackjack. He and his wads of hard-earned money are welcome anywhere downtown, but he likes the Nevada Club best. Says it reminds him most of the old days. Lung Fung's reminds me of the old days. I like to go in and remember the voices from the back booth: "You cheat! You are always cheating!" "Now calm down before you have a stroke. Hey, you can't trump! Hearts haven't been broken."

◊

Chuckles the chauffeur deposits me at the curb on the other side of Virginia Street from Lung Fung's and Landrums then peels out on the dust in the gutter, hangs a U-ie and speeds back the way we came. I thanked him—I did. And he nearly ripped my arm off before I could let go of the door handle. Hope he goes home and takes a pleasant pill. What

111

Johnny sees in that guy ... Probably a matter of it takes one to know one.

There's a decent gap in the traffic but I charge across anyway because it's minutes before six. I'd hate to miss anything juicy. No time for the moo goo right now. Too bad. I'm starving.

Lung's not around tonight, but I still get a royal welcome. I swear there must be a picture of me on the job application. I can hear Lung saying, "Susan Anne, she Dave Murrow daughter. You don't know Dave, maybe. Long time ago. But I tell you, they family. You see Susan Anne, you treat like family. No messing around. No charge anytime." He never takes my money for food. I make up for it by overtipping the hell out of his staff. And giving a buck here and there to the little kids who are always running around.

At Pop's funeral, Lung's whole family, and it seemed like everyone who worked for him past and present showed up. They came into the church together and tried to sit in the very back pews. But I remember a whole group of guys—fire department and police department both—going back there and bringing all of them up to where they and their families were sitting. The women from Lung Fung's brought flowers, all white. Chrysanthemums. Gardenias. I heard Lung weeping during the service. And one of the clearest things in my mind from that day: I heard him say, "Damn cheater" as he laid a king of hearts on the closed casket. These things you see and hear and you don't forget. I wish I'd taken that card. Don't know what happened to it.

"I hope it's not an inconvenience," I say to the waitress I've never seen before but who is holding a big red menu out to me and smiling like we're old friends. "I want to hold off on dinner. What I need right now is to go through the kitchen to the back door. Would that be alright with you?"

"Sure, sure. I take you," she says and goes ahead of me, shouting sweaty cooks out of our way. Good hostess; she's going to make sure she walks me somewhere.

"Thanks," I say. "I'll order in a minute."

"Take your time. No hurry." She glares at the cooks who are staring at me and they go back to work. The smell here is heaven. Flames and smoke and steam rise all around. Chunks of flora and fauna zing through the air. The floor's thick with sticky grease and beside the door there's a garbage can full of an aromatic blend of decomposing animal and vegetable parts. I'm going to try not to think about this feature of the meal I wish I had time to eat.

"You guys mind if I smoke?" I ask when I get to the door they've got propped open with a cinder block. They shake their heads. Then I notice there's a carpet of butts right outside. And three blue dinette chairs. An old fruit crate to use as a table or to put your feet up on. I stand a bit inside the doorway where I can flick my ashes outside but not be seen from the back of Landrums across Arroyo Street which runs between Landrums and Lung Fung's.

The small parking area where I'm standing runs back to a dirt embankment. Beyond that is a vacant lot full of weeds. To my left are four parked cars. Those take up all the spaces against the block wall of an electronics repair shop next to Lung's. The wall runs back to the embankment. I'm hemmed in on two sides; my clear ways out are through Lung Fung's or onto Arroyo.

On the Landrums side, there's the cafe, another small parking lot in back with only one car in it and a two-story four-plex I can see the top floor of behind a six-foot wooden fence. My pals from the jail house will either come in from one of two ways: Holcomb or Virginia, but I only have a clear view of Holcomb. In the short time I've had to examine my surroundings I have seen no unnecessary lurkers, no cruising cars. The buffer behind me—all those cooks with all those sharp knives—relives me of having to look over my shoulder. I can worry about what's directly in front of me. Chinese cooking will take care of the rear. I check my Timex. The show should start any minute now.

On cue the two prompt slimeballs come strolling up from Holcomb Street. A stoned bounce to their steps. They keep their heads down, hands in their pockets, and groove into the lot behind Landrums. Go over to lean against the back wall of the cafe, each propping his left foot behind him. They light up cigarettes. Scoop the hair out of their eyes. The sky's starting to get dark. Actually, it's starting to get orange the way the sun's going down tonight. Over to the east, the way I'm facing, the clouds are going pink and purple with shades of gray. The wind's died down quite a bit from this morning which is always nice. Usually it starts to rev up at sundown.

A pearl white Corvette roars up from the Virginia Street direction and pulls in at the curb next to Landrums. The driver revs the engine once, loud, cuts it, and gets out. Johnny. Same outfit. Shirt still open. He and my chauffeur must have passed each other somewhere along the route from Johnny's casa to Reno. If ole Duke even noticed, I doubt he gave a good rat's ass. Johnny wouldn't bother noticing.

He takes a fairly conspicuous look around before sidling over to his buddies. They're a good head taller than he is now that they're standing at attention. Johnny's upper body leans toward them with an intensity that expects good answers. Not smart ones. Not right ones. Just good ones—the ones he wants to hear. He has his hands on his hips like Sergeant Carter listening to Gomer, impatiently waiting for them to finish with their tale of woe. Blondy is the spokesman as usual. Acne Boy's just there for moral support. Blondy talks with his hands, his whole body getting into the act of telling about their adventure last night. I can see when he's at the part about me

114

because he put one hand out about so high and then with both of them draws an air picture of a lot of hair.

Then Blondy gives Johnny something. Could be my card or the money or both. Must be my card because Johnny looks at it, rips it up, and throws it in the guy's face. Then Blondy hands him what must be the money which Johnny stuffs in his pants pocket. And comes out with his trusty switchblade. He lunges at the loser who's done the most talking and jabs him repeatedly in the gut. Just like that. Acne Boy stands there for a second, frozen by what he's watching.

"Call the police!" I yell over my shoulder at the cooks who just look at one another. "Call the police now!" I yell louder. I draw my .357 and run out across the street.

Acne Boy finally gets his feet to move and takes off toward the fence at the back of Landrums parking lot with Johnny hot on his tail. They go one after the other over the fence into the yard of the four-plex. Acne Boy practically vaults it clean. Johnny has to jump up onto a trash can to make it. Still not too shabby a move. I decide to run down Arroyo and catch them coming out at Holcomb. I can hear running. I can hear tumbling. The loser is yelling for help. And then he's just yelling. Then nothing.

I reach the corner just as Johnny does, coming full speed toward me, headed for his car. He plows into me with his arms blocker-crossed in front of him. Doesn't even look at me—I'm just a thing in his way. I fall backward into the street on my ass. It knocks the wind out of me, not to mention hurting like hell. This is going to leave a bruise. Johnny scrams to the 'vette and he's inside by the time I pick myself up off the pavement. He guns the engine. The headlights pop up and come on. The tires smoke, and he's fishtailing in my direction. I roll behind the corner of the fence, raise my gun and fire. I hear the bullet strike metal. On that fiberglass beast, I must have hit some window trim or a mirror. Nice shooting, Flack. The 'vette's rear quarter smashes in the fence just in front of where I'm hiding. I roll out of the way as boards fly. The car's still swerving out of control and takes out the street sign on the corner. Johnny makes a skidding left turn onto Holcomb as the sign spins out into the street, sparks flying.

I fire from where I have gracefully landed on my ass again and hit the left taillight. Then he's out of range. Zero to sixty in five seconds flat? Makes for a smooth getaway. He'll need to get off the main roads before he's too much farther into town, driving the way he is and the car looking the way it does. My choice would be to head out Mill to Kietzke and then north as fast and as far as I had gas to go.

I pick myself up, dust off, cuss myself for missing—twice—and limp back toward Lung Fung's. The body on the ground behind Landrums hasn't moved, isn't going to move by the looks of things. Probably the same story for the body behind the fence. So much for the two losers I'd paid to be my friends for life just a few hours ago. I was hoping to get more out of them than a one-night stand.

By now there's more activity than this neighborhood's seen in a long while. One of the tenants at the four-plex has probably called the cops to complain about the noise. I figure it'll be better for my own future if I put in a call to them, too. The cooks are all gawking at the door when I get back.except one who's screaming Chinese into the grimy phone. I jerk the receiver out of his hand and hang up. I'm shaking bad enough to have to start over three times before I get dial in the number to the cops. I ask for McMannis, and he's there. His lucky day still. I give him the details even though there are sirens already on the way. Looks like my day's caught up with me big time. I've got plenty of explaining to do, more than a few feathers to unruffle. And it's not even all the way dark yet.

Chapter 12

"Flack? Hey, Flack, you awake?"

"What else?" I'd been staring at the ceiling since ten o'clock, last call for bedtime for the mob in the Larson house. I'd heard the phone ring. Figured Red'd be knocking. I always welcomed what that knock meant.

Timmy and I had been living at Red and Edie's for almost two years since Mom died. Timmy adjusted to all of the noise and headstrong individuals in the family by becoming unnaturally quiet, obedient, and listless. I just kept on keeping on. What else was new? We both arrived in this situation pretty crapped out, having given all we had for too many worthless months trying to convince Mom she needed to survive. We were good. We cleaned our rooms. We helped her into bed when she couldn't even find it. But Mom had slipped away from us like we never mattered. I stared at the ceiling most of the night every night since then, hoping to figure out where a person's caring went when they gave up like that. Probably would have been best if I hadn't come to any conclusions which I ultimately did. In this strange house full of maniacs—and with Timmy headed down the same road as

Mom at the ripe old age of eleven—I could only think, "Here we go again."

The insomnia I swear I was born with had only gotten worse after Pop was killed. Then after Mom . . . Red, who said he used to fall asleep the second his head hit the pillow, was having problems, too. So he didn't mind when he got called out of bed in the middle of the night. In the explosion that killed Pop, Red, who was going in behind him, lost the hearing in his right ear and along with it, all hope of another peaceful night's sleep. He couldn't stop thinking he should have done something to prevent Pop's death. Warned him somehow. Predicted what was coming. Gone into the warehouse first. Red was right there. Says it all the time: "Right there." He'd watched as Pop's body had flown backward through the air like it was nothing – the front all in flames. It was just one of those freaky things that happens, just enough to take Pop out of the game and to keep Red awake all night reliving how he'd failed a friend.

"Want to have a look at something with me?" Red whispered. He wiggled one of my feet to get me moving without waking his two daughters who shared their room with me—like anything short of an atomic bomb blast could wake those two.

"Sure. Got nothing else to do. Give me a sec."

He went out and closed the door most of the way, leaving me just enough light to see by. I jumped into my jeans, tennies, and a sweatshirt. Tried to calm my hair down a little but ended up mashing a Giants ballcap down on the unruly mess.

"What'cha got?" I asked, squinting at the bright kitchen lights.

"House fire. Up on Skyline. Started in the basement."

"Nice neighborhood."

"Yeah. House was one of the big ones. Boys are just mopping up."

"Damn, the place'll be soaked, and I've got a hole in my shoe."

I was fourteen years old and going out with Red at three-thirty in the morning to check out a possible arson. After the warehouse thing, Red had gotten "busted down," as he put it, to inspector—partly because of his hearing but partly because he survived, dragged Pop's body out, and got the commendation that bumped him up in rank. Being one of the higher-ups didn't make him all that happy. Though he was grateful still to be part of the department, he missed being a fireman on the line. One of the bad asses, the first on the scene. Now, he made more money, had some authority, didn't get called out of a warm bed too often. He was a lot safer, but he felt put out to pasture. He was always last on the scene now and about the only fun he had with his work was taking me with him, showing me the ropes: when is a fire not an ordinary fire.

Red made coffee and salami sandwiches, our usual. We had a red plaid cosmetic case of Edie's that we used as a lunch box.

"We got Oreos?" I asked. I shook a Lucky Strike out of the pack on the table. Rule in the Larson house, down from Edie herself, was that you had to be fourteen before you could smoke. I took it up as soon as I came of age. Timmy, who was only thirteen, and three of the Larson kids were still too young. I found smoking passed quite a bit of time when you were wide-awake thinking at night. I picked up Edie's brand as my own just because her Luckies were always around. Red smoked Viceroys. The only one in the house who did.

"I got your Oreos," he said, adding a wax paper packet of cookies to the lunch box. "Ready?"

"As I'll ever be," I told him casually like I did every time. These investigations were the only things I could get excited about anymore. It was a huge relief to have something to do

119

and a thrill to go into these places where I knew I wasn't supposed to be. But I tried to act like it wasn't a big deal.

Red handed me the Thermos of coffee.

"You going to be warm enough?" he asked.

I stubbed out my smoke. "Warm enough."

That was the last time I went out on a fire with Red. The last time for Red, too. I never meant for him to know the shit that happened to me under his roof. What I was willing to put up with to stay close to this man—the one who told only me how Pop hadn't died right off; how Red had held him, watched him die. But Red found out my secret. It happened too fast. Like an explosion. I tried to tell him it didn't matter. But it mattered too much, and it changed everything in one day.

Chapter 13

I sit down on one of the blue dinette chairs outside. Lay my gun on the fruit crate; the police'll want to have a look at it. One of the cooks offers me a cigarette; two others try to give me a light. A kindly waitress brings out a pot of tea and a load of little handless cups on a round, cork-topped tray. I move the gun to my lap so she can set the tray on the fruit crate. She produces a pint of Black Velvet from her apron pocket. Several hands reach for cups. She fills them all and one for herself and one for me. I lift my cup to them, and we drink in silence.

Gunfire has a tendency to clear out places like restaurants. As I was walking back toward Lung Fung's, I saw a little huddle of customers on the sidewalk, some of them clutching their red napkins, peeking around the corner. When they actually saw that what they thought they'd heard going on outside was true, they vanished, and there probably won't be many more takers for dinner at the House of Lung Fung for the next several hours. The Landrums customers, on the other hand, came out, took a look around, shrugged their shoulders, and went back inside to finish their omelets.

Sirens are closing in on the scene. If I had my car, I'd think twice about staying put—I'd take off after that Johnny-punk in

121

a heartbeat. In the GTO, I could probably catch him, too. Love to get my hands on his skinny neck right now. But before I choked the life out of him, I'd make him tell me what he's into that's juicy for Mona to be his steady girl til she gets it. Can't be the usual things. She'd have thought of those already. This must be something with pizzazz—a cut above the world of everyday crime because, crimewise, we've got nothing but latitude here in Nevada. A virtual buffet of nefarious pursuits that *aren't* illegal. We simply don't dot our i's out of sheer orneriness.

Five patrol cars pull up from different directions, lights flashing. An ambulance swings in from the wrong way on one-way Center Street. My waitress serves me another healthy shot of Black Velvet, then the entire staff of Lung Fung's disappears into the restaurant. They'll claim to have seen nothing, no one, never, no way. Hard at work. I understand. Every one of them has something, past or present, that doesn't need to be talked about. Especially to the police. These people who have offered me their company and their hospitality since I was a kid will turn on the blank Chinese stare that white Americans expect, and the police will have no luck getting behind it. Won't get a thing out of me as it pertains to them, either.

Rodgers and Harney are two of the cops who show up, thank you very much. But the other uniforms, I've never seen before. Getting old, Flack. Not too many of Pop's connections run around in blue anymore. They're all in plain clothes, running things from the station. Or they've retired. Or became sheriffs in exotic places like Wendover or Battle Mountain were the biggest problems are the fights that break out between miners and tramp construction workers after the eagle flies on Fridays. Rodgers and Harney are getting pretty old to be in blue themselves, but I think they like the action too much to go for the promotions they've deserved for years.

Seems like neither one of them is too wild about the possibility that getting ambitious might break up the team. They've seen a lot together, backed each other up. Must be nice to have someone like that to rely on. Must be nice to want to see the same old face day after day.

Rodgers is dispatching four uniformed cops over to the Landrums side of the street. They're drawing their guns and looking like they wish there was somewhere else they were supposed to be. The four of them form kind of a protective semi-circle and move across the street. Locating that first body is like finding an Easter egg smack dab on the sidewalk, and they move together like a school of fish to take a look. They yell for the ambulance guys who are already bringing a stretcher and a bunch of medical stuff from the back of their rig.

Harney walks up to me and doesn't look pleased.

"Hey," I say, pointing my cigarette at the apartment house. "Tell those guys there's another one. Over the fence."

"Rodgers!" Harney yells. He makes a swooping motion with his arm to indicate what I've told him. Rodgers picks out two uniforms to go over there with him.

"You responsible for any of this, Flack?"

"If you mean the bodies, no. I mean, not directly. I mean, I did see it go down." I know I'm stumbling all over myself. I stub out my cigarette and brace myself to come pretty clean. I say, "It's the two screw-ups from my office last night. The ones you and Rodgers hauled in."

"The ones you never filled out a report on?"

"Yeah, and I'm sorry about that. There's sort of a lot you don't know about last night. I'll get to it, I promise . . ."

"Right, like you said you'd follow us to the station."

"I said I'm sorry, okay? I had some things to take care of."

He's standing over me with his arms crossed. I feel like I'm in the principal's office.

"Keep going," he says.

"I knew those guys were coming here tonight, but I didn't know it was for them to end up dead. They told me they were supposed to meet some Mexican who hired them for a job."

"And this job had something to do with you?"

"Yeah, they thought I had this thing they were hired to get back."

"What thing?"

"Baseball cards." Had to tell him the truth, didn't I? As crazy as it sounded. Hammerstein reacts by walking a few steps away from me and wiping his hand over his face. Muttering words I can't hear clearly. He comes back, adjusts his hat. Doesn't say a word. Just motions "and?" with his left hand.

"Sounds crazy but that's what they said. Said the dude who hired them gave them each a hundred bucks to follow this guy who'd ripped him off."

"Oh, now this would be the stiff you sic-ed McMannis on this morning *and*, I might add, ran out on filing that report, too."

"That would be the cadaver in question."

"What's the connection between you and him and these baseball cards?"

"The guy shows up at my office last night. Drunk. Out of the blue. And I never found out what he wanted. Those two losers ran him off before they trashed my place. Then you took them to jail, and the dead body appeared in my swivel chair some time between when we'd all left last night and when I got back this morning. Right around 10:30."

"Get back to the baseball cards."

I light another cigarette. "That's what they told me they wanted when we talked this morning."

"You come down and bail them out?"

"Not exactly. I knew you wouldn't hold them past ten . . ."

"Grady didn't let you back there again, did he?"

"No, sir. Grady set me straight on pestering him at work." Like I said, I'm coming *pretty* clean.

"Okay. You wait around for these two to walk, and that's when they tell you what they were looking for?"

"Correct."

"And you have these cards?"

"Not on me."

"You do have them?"

"Not if you don't have a search warrant."

He takes another little walk away from me to wipe his face and mutter again. I drink the rest of the Black Velvet in my teacup. I'm going to tell him as much of the truth as I want him to know. I'm going to try not to fib quite as bad as I've had to since last night – I owe him that much. But until I know more about this situation myself, I'd rather skirt a few of the more meaty issues.

Hammerstein and I are in a bit of a stand-off when Rodgers jogs toward us across Arroyo. A man that age wearing that many donuts and clanking hardware shouldn't set it all in motion at once.

"Got two bodies. One there, one by the apartments. Stabbed. They're the two we picked up at her place last night."

"I know," says Harney, glaring at me.

"Evening, Flack," says Rodgers. "Hey, that was lousy of you not to show up last night."

"We've been over that," says Hammerstein.

"What were those two doing here? Hey, and while we're at it, what are you doing here?" Rodgers asks me.

"I'll fill you in later," says Harney. "You get a look at this Mexican, Flack?"

"Yeah, I did. Took a shot at the son of a bitch when he tried to run over me with his car before he split. Here, you'll probably want this." I hold out the Python. Rodgers slides his

125

thick finger through the trigger guard and lets the gun dangle. He takes it over and puts it on the front seat of the squad car.

"Did you hit him?" Harney asks.

"No, missed him but hit his car. Twice. White, hard-top 'vette. About a '68, '69, I think. License W12876. First shot hit the roof above the windshield. A few more inches down and I'd've got him. Second one blew out the left taillight."

Harney looks startled, which is unusual.

"Give me that license number again," he says.

I tell him.

He takes his notepad out of his chest pocket and leafs through the pages. He stays on top of details like nobody I've ever seen. Got a memory that won't quit. Dates, names, stuff he reads. How much stuff costs.

"Damn. Damn." He's staring at the paper. "Describe this man."

"Kind of scrawny, maybe goes 145, 150 pounds. 5'9" tops. Black hair. Long. Straight. Dark eyes, set wide. Almond-shaped. Beak for a nose. Good looking in a sleazy way. He was wearing white pants and a red shirt, unbuttoned."

"Damn."

"What 'damn,' damn it?"

"Johnny . . ."

He knows the guy's name is Johnny.

"Johnny Ruggerio."

Ruggerio. Shit, I know that name as well as anybody and it ain't Mexican. "He's a *Ruggerio*?"

"Oh Jesus, Flack. You shot a *Ruggerio*?"

"I missed, damn it, I missed a Ruggerio."

"He see you?"

Did he? I don't know. It all happened so fast, like they say on the t.v. news. I do know that if he recognized me, I'll have the entire Ruggerio armed forces to worry about. I wish that waitress with the Black Velvet would come back.

I light another cigarette from the butt of the last one and offer the pack to Harney. He quit a year ago, but I might as well help him make an exception under the circumstances. Ruggerio. Their money built gambling in northern Nevada back in the twenties. That and their willingness to take out all objects animate or inanimate that posed even the remotest threat to their absolute rulership of the gaming industry here. The messiest moments of the family's business dealings were ancient history by the mid-forties, but you'd be stupid not to notice the force of their influence still very much at work. They donate to this and that and sponsor this and that – very philanthropic toward the cause of civic betterment in Washoe County. All of us have benefited in some way from their contributions to starting up the bus system or building new hospital wings at Washoe Med and St. Mary's or giving up hundreds of acres of land for schools and parks. We tend not ask embarrassing – or dangerous – questions when a Ruggerio "suggests" certain things ought to happen that would be good for their businesses. Or when a stray body in a three-piece suit washes up on the shore at Pyramid Lake. The Ruggerios *are* northern Nevada, and we all know we owe them a thousand times over for our livelihoods. Hell, for some of us, we might owe them just for letting us live in the first place.

Now's my turn to say, "Damn." Damn Mona. She might have said something. Damn me – I didn't ask. The way he was dressed, I thought he might be a lounge entertainer. Or a coke dealer. Upstart movie mogul in his vacation house? Not for one second did I think that he'd be one of the offsprings of the offsprings of Antonio and Sophia Ruggerio.

I stand up. "Damn," I say to Harney, grinding my smoke into the pavement with the toe of my boot.

The ambulance crew has gathered up the bodies, and Rodgers goes to talk to the driver. The ambulance drives away without lights or sirens as Rodgers hefts his way back to me and Hammerstein.

Rodgers says, "Whoever killed them did a nasty job on those two. Knew just the right spots to hit to get a guy to bleed out fast. Hey, you smoking again, Harney?"

Harney takes a long drag and looks stunned. "It was Ruggerio. Johnny Ruggerio."

Rodgers looks at me and looks back at Harney and back at me. "Damn," he says.

I ask Harney, "What've you got in your notes about him?"

"Our Johnny's trying to branch out. Horses. Thoroughbred racers. Got a stable out on Franktown Road. Hired some trainers and jockeys away from Santa Anita, a couple of other places. Wants to build a track at his stable. The whole she-bang. Grandstand, club house, betting. Everything first-rate, of course. Well, his neighbors out there in Washoe Valley are having a conniption. Don't want the noise and the traffic, or the clientele. Plus the fact that Johnny's place is part in Washoe County and part in Carson City. Politics and taxes, you know? Strange bedfellows. In the past month, there have been some 'incidents' out there. Vandalism, burglaries, a couple of assaults. At both Johnny's place and the neighbors'. Nothing involving Johnny directly, of course. This stuff appears to be going on between his staff and the surrounding property owners mostly. But we have been watching it escalate, and it is starting to get ugly."

Yeah, I think. As ugly as a naked corpse with a giant needle in his arm.

"Let me see if I can complete this picture," I say. "Johnny's pissed off about not getting his way and as soon as he personally decides to get in the middle of it, there's going to be a war."

Rodgers nods. "You got it."

"And I took a couple of shots at him and then i.d.'ed him to the cops?"

"Yep."

"Well, I guess there's only one question left to ask."

"What?"

"How soon can I get my gun back?"

Chapter 14

There are only a few ways to get me to sit down and give a statement for the cops, one of them is if they have my precious Colt Python and I want it back. After I accompany Rogers and Hammerstein to the station, finally dictate my three official reports to a sleepy stenographer, argue a roomful of insistent lawmen into letting me surrender the evidence in my possession tomorrow, *and* talk the captain himself into giving me back my gun, Rodgers and Harney drive me to my car at the Holiday Inn. Not bad for a night's work.

On the way, they speculate about the cosmic meaning of baseball cards worth killing for. They decide to leave it that the rich are different and when you have money, you can be as eccentric as a split rail fence. They're heavily into the next topic—what aspects of a player or his game would rank him as a member of Johnny's card collection—while I'm busy trying to tune them out so that I can reach conclusions to questions of my own. I'm bushed, dead on my feet. I could drop. I wish that could still be true when I flop into bed, shut my eyes, and the neverending rerun of my life starts again.

Knowing exactly who I've been dealing with the past couple of days has rearranged my thinking about several parts of this puzzle. I know now that wad of hundreds in the stocking is nothing stolen. Just a trinket, a trademark mannerism. The hundred dollar chip from Crystal Bay Club likewise means nothing: Crystal Bay was one of the family's first casinos. The chip is probably just some loose change he gave Michael. Hope it wasn't for luck. I can go ahead and turn over most of the evidence I've been withholding–except the cash, of course. That'll put the department in such a mad frenzy of fingerprinting and cataloging, they ought to be out of my hair for a good long while. All I will be hanging onto are Mike's notebook and the pawn ticket, both of which I sort of neglected to mention in my statements. I'm keeping the notebook because it's personal, but the item to be claimed with the pawn ticket is almost certainly what Johnny's all hot about. The cops don't need to know about that.

"We'll wait and make sure your car starts," Rodgers says as we pull into the packed parking lot at the Holiday Inn. Such a gent. I'm having a rare wimpy moment, so I appreciate that they're going to stand guard over me. There are plenty more places for bad guys to be hiding now. Plenty more cars to box me in.

"Thanks a lot, you guys," I say as I take a look around, trying not to look like I'm taking a look around. "I'll see you tomorrow when I drop off the stuff."

"It's our day off, Flack, but you damn well better do it. We don't want to have to hunt you down and get rough with you," Harney says and laughs.

"Oh, I'm scared – real scared. Bye-bye, boys." Just darling: they even have the same day off.

The GTO fires right up, and Harney gives me the "cool, baby" circle-sign with his thumb and forefinger. I nod back to him. Cops appreciate good cars. This one's almost there. Wheels are next on my shopping list now that all the engine work is done. Baby moons, I think. Then new upholstery. After that, my GTO will be extremely cherry.

They move the squad car. I can back up, and they follow me out of the parking lot. I make a right on Sixth—which isn't the way I go home—but I know they're going left and I've seen enough of them for one day, two if you count last night.

It's too late for the pawn shop to be open, but I'll swing by there first thing in the morning on my way to the office. And since it is late and there's no one around, I burn rubber through three gears taking off from the light at Wells and Fourth. There's a little chatter in the clutch. Got to have it looked at.

Chapter 15

I slept last night. The real thing. Like a babe from three a.m. all the way to six. Slept like I deserved it, and though I don't feel quite like a million bucks, I do feel mildly more than usual like going out and tackling my little corner of the world. As soon as I've had coffee and a shower.

I throw on clean Levi's, my town boots—change my mind and switch to my riding boots, and the less wrinkled of my two white dress shirts. I'm feeling strangely awake, I even dab some eye shadow, mascara and blush onto the appropriate places and wonder why I don't do this more often: it's good to be a girl. I think I'll go for some of that hooker-red lipstick, too. A mouth like a crimson gash. I read that somewhere. I grab as sweater and Pop's jacket. Pop's jacket—my thinking gear.

Outside the trailer door, a gorgeous morning surrounds the quiet trailer park. I sit down on the metal step to drink my coffee. Look at the paper. Campus unrest. Sit-ins. Strikes. Marches. Poor, rich babies. As if Daddy and Mommy footing the bill for four years of carefree partying isn't enough, the folks now have to come up with bail, too. It's still a bit uncomfortably cool this early, but it'll warm up today, I can feel it. A teaser day we might as well enjoy. Summer's still a long way off. But for now the wind is calm. Sun's out. Birdies chirping in the greening-up cottonwoods. The kind of day when it's a bad idea to rush into indoor problems.

I've got my methods for getting to the bottom of things—most of which look like there's no real work being done. But gluing your nose to the ground or sticking every little scrap under a microscope is for amateurs who haven't figured out how to tell what's important and want to feel good bragging about how damn busy they are. I'm more the back-burner type. I learned pretty fast to walk away before I confuse myself. Shake out the cobwebs and see what the near-sighted and the frantic miss. Perspective. How are you going to get it if you're all hunched over or squinted up? It's a trick Red taught me: stay on an even keel or get back that way quick. Save the fine points for the very end.

I'm not expected at Johnny's til after six. The item waiting to be picked up with the pawn ticket I found in his baseball cards isn't going anywhere. Never known a Shylock to give up anything without a claim check. Murders, mayhem and curiosity aside, it's a beautiful day, confusion is just around the bend, and I can think of no better head-straightener than a ride in the wide, open spaces with some quality companionship. I keep her out at Hope Springs Stables.

Rockalee's my tall bay mare. Too tall for me, really. But she is a thing of beauty. Fashionably narrow through the nose. Long legged and damn fast. Smooth as the GTO at high speeds. Only problem is she's just not very bright. She forgets how to behave like a lady if I don't exercise her legs and her brain at least every three or four days. The only thing she always seems able to recall without my gentle reminders is how to find her way back to the stable. When I haven't ridden her for a while, she'll spend the first half hour out whinnying to her pals and jerking to the right. Once that half hour's up her natural stupidity kicks in and she completely forgets she has a home, she struts out through the sagebrush on those long, beautiful legs of hers like she owns the place. Then as we're coming back and we're within a half hour of the barn, she suddenly remembers where she gets fed and yanks at the reins again. She's a great ride, but I definitely don't love her for her mind.

I toss the lukewarm dregs of my coffee onto my gravel front yard, dunk the newspaper into the trash can by the door and start loading my tack into the trunk of the GTO. Don't like to keep much of my stuff out at Hope Springs though secure storage space comes with the price of boarding. It's not that I worry about anything getting stolen; I just find that being able to look over from my bed at a saddle and a fly rod waiting by the door is a healthy reminder that there are at least two other things worth doing besides work. Then guess what I use my recreation time to think about? What else is there? Work or Timmy. You choose.

About a mile from home—The Doors' "Roadhouse Blues" blasting on the eight-track—I remember I forgot to bring the evidence I'm supposed to turn over to the cops today. I cuss the damn inconvenience of being the good citizen that I am and turn around and head back home.

I take the front grille off the speaker and gather up Michael Parker's odd assortment of personal effects. Damn, the baseball cards. I'm tempted to keep the Mickey Mantle, but decide it'd just be a reminder of this Johnny-thing which is shaping up to be something I'll want to forget. I hate having to take Mike's crap with me while I'm trying to clear my head about circumstances concerning him. I shove it all without another inspection into a grocery bag and chuck it into the trunk with the saddle. Out of sight, out of mind for the moment. I switch the tunes in the tape player from The Doors to BB King. He's singing with this new chick. Great voice I'd never heard before I heard this song: Bonnie Raitt. A redhead, of course. I crank it up.

I bomb north on 395 until I come to the new freeway section they've been building since the dawn of time and still haven't finished. Here, I get off at the orange barricades and weave slow as hell through the side streets clear over to the Interstate where I can then zoom east. When and if the new part of 395 ever opens, I plan to be the first person to drive onto it and once there, I will get down on my knees and kiss the blessed pavement. My drive from home to points north – which is all of Reno and Sparks and where I do ninety percent of my business – will be a breeze when these eight, delicious miles come into my life. Moana Lane to Golden Valley without stopping. Yee-haw. But for now, I creep past the construction site where groups of three guys lean on shovels every hundred or so yards, supervising one guy who's working himself up to doing some work. We poor south-of-towners can only hope that someday soon the almighty construction company will have overcharged the taxpayers enough to consider their job done and let us the hell onto *our* freeway.

At the stable, Rockalee – Rocky if she's behaving – shies away from me until I whip out the red apple lure that works every time. While she chomps and slobbers, I hitch up the saddle. She's shedding her winter coat, short hairs flying everywhere, and her mane and tail are in need of serious grooming. Full of stickers and weeds and tangles. I'll be paying Anita to keep Rocky spruced up this month since I'm stealing valuable time as it is from bigger matters. I've got more to do today than most people do in a week. But this isn't the first time, and another thing Red taught me is that staying all tense and anxious only makes things take longer than they should.

I lead Rockalee out of the corral and around to the abandoned, metal truck racks that I use as a ladder to get up on her. You should see me out on the desert trying to get back in the saddle if I get down to pee or just want to walk around for a while. I ought to teach her to hold out a foreleg like they train elephants to do so I could step up on her knee and swing into the saddle. As it is, once I'm down, I have to keep running and swinging until I get back up. Very embarrassing. But climbing a truck rack isn't exactly sexy. Short people with tall horses do what they have to do. She side-steps once I'm on, getting used to my weight, and after she mellows out as much as I can expect her to, I fight her through the brush while she goes through her whinnying, right-turning routine.

Rockalee and I head south up Hope Springs Canyon, the namesake of the Hope Springs Stables. This time of year, there may be a trickle of water and a little green vegetation to see up there. We had an average winter, and the Springs shouldn't dry up until about the middle of June depending on how soon the weather gets hot and if it stays hot. You never can tell. I couldn't call myself a true desert rat–and I do with pride–if I missed my chance to see the two weirdest things you can see in the desert: wet and green. I struggle to keep Rocky's head turned in the direction of the canyon until finally I feel her amnesia kicking in. Now I can relax, smoke, enjoy the ride . . . and think about work.

I've got a tiger by the tail with my friend Johnny. He must be a throw-back – doesn't look like any of the Ruggerios I've ever met. For Italians, they're almost all blond and blue-eyed. But along comes Johnny who looks like the stereotype. I sure thought he was Mexican, though – never crossed my mind to wonder otherwise after Heckle and Jeckle led me astray. He looked like I expected him to look, that's all. But he wasn't who I expected to meet, that's for sure.

I did some work for the Ruggerios while I was part of Recovery Specialists. They're the kind of client you collect an estimated half-payment from upfront because you will spend at least six months chasing down the balance. I figured out from them how rich people get and stay rich: they never pay their bills. At Recovery Specialists, we *had* to work for the Ruggerios; it'd be small business suicide not to. When the Ruggerios talk, people listen so if they're going to be talking about you, you want them to say something nice. Since the Ruggerios own or are part-owners in eight casinos, they have more than their share of problems with employees ripping them off which means plenty of work for Recovery Specialists. In all the Ruggerio cases I was part of, I knew they couldn't begin to catch the amounts of money being stolen from them. Wanting to catch the crooks appeared to me to be a matter of principle. I appreciate principles wherever and in whoever I find them – even in rich gangster descendants of gangsters. I enjoyed the work I did for them and let our secretary worry about collecting the money. One thing is sure: I never thought I'd be dealing with a member of their family again this soon. And in such a different way.

Interesting proposition grandson Johnny has dreamed up: a horse track out on Franktown Road. It is pretty out there and it's good horse property, too. Grassy. But the wind screams hard nearly all the time out there in Washoe Valley, I can't imagine expecting people to sit out in it to watch a horse race. The wind would make things interesting, though – watching the horses struggling against a forty mile per hour zephyr down the home stretch. I doubt there'd be many speed records set at Johnny's track, but it might turn out some powerful animals.

From the gambling point of view, a race track makes sense—carrying on the family tradition. Something else to bet on, in and out of their casinos. It's a unique idea, not all that far out, and full of potential for payoffs that would interest local lawmakers. If it were me planning a project like that, I'd sure be worried less about my neighbors and more about starting a tax war between two counties that would cost a bundle to clear up and an eternity to get okay-ed.

Then there's what might be the biggest problem of all: Washoe Lake likes to seep into the Valley pastureland and form mushy pools in surprising places most of the year. Doesn't seem to me like any amount of engineering could keep a track flat and dry on land that likes to be marshy. But who am I? I can't even balance a checkbook. I suppose if anybody in Reno could afford to hire enough of the right people to figure out how to get such a job done, it'd be a Ruggerio.

The animal-nature of Johnny's project explains how Michael Parker came to be killed with a veterinary syringe, but it doesn't explain why or who. The killers weren't the two losers Johnny offed last night; they were sitting in jail when the deed was done. It wasn't Johnny either. If he himself had come after Mikey, there's a strong chance I would not be riding the range on a day that's warming up so pleasantly and fast I take off Pop's jacket and my sweater. And I've seen how Johnny prefers to do his killing. I think whoever killed Mike was not part of Johnny's plans. This drug thing looks like someone else's m.o. An independent operator? Someone with a grudge? Wouldn't be out of the question. Jealous girlfriend? Someone on a political payroll? How could I think such a thing? In Nevada? But on the bright side, here once again we see a Ruggerio doing his part for the employment picture: hiring a guy to follow me to see if I'm worth hiring and hiring two more guys to follow the guy he hired to follow me. Sharing the wealth.

Rockalee and I pass in and out of shadows in the canyon. It's still cold where the sun's not shining. A thin trickle of water that is all Hope Springs amounts to even on the best year. It runs down a little gully between banks covered with short, bright grasses and white, daisy-type flowers that survive only as far as a faint dampness extends and for only as long as the snow-melt feeds the Springs. This is what I needed to see today. Something natural, growing. Nothing to do with people who I've decided as a group have lost every shred of respect for their place in nature. On my rides, I kid myself that all of this beautiful, empty space will be left alone. That people on dirt bikes and dune buggies or with house plans under their arms won't ever come along and mess it up. But I'm already seeing it happen.

We arrive at my favorite spot to sit and smoke by the Springs. Might even soak my toes. There are a couple of scrawny willows up here that I can pretend are real trees if I lie down. The wall of the canyon is good and steep on this side, too, which makes a handy ramp for me to climb off and on my too tall horse. I let Rockalee's reins hang after I got off. She likes it here and has forgotten about making a break for home. She immediately puts her head down and starts tearing up the tender grass I've been admiring, her hooves sinking into the wet sand. So much for people – and their critters – not messing up a place.

I lie back against the slope of the canyon in a sunny spot, listen to the grasshoppers snapping around and to the almost unnoticeable gurgle of the springs. A hawk flies over and screeches. I'd like to stay here all day. All my life. Nah, probably better just to visit. To leave some places special so they're there whenever we need them. And best kept as secrets.

When I was a kid Pop would take all of us out to "get lost." On purpose. Comes automatically to me. Dad used to get us lost on purpose, in town or out. He said you can't find anything new if you don't get lost once in a while. Gets me thinking about the time we found an old mining operation when we were out desert-ratting in the truck one day. We'd been bouncing along a washed out dirt road near Wabuska.

Timmy and me were riding in back, watching and eating the cloud of dust we were raising along with our Oreos. Couple of times we bounced hard enough that we flew up in the air. The landings were pretty hard, but we were laughing our butts off. We could see Dad's arm pointing out this or that he wanted Mom to see, and we also knew that if he was pointing, he wasn't paying all that much attention to the road ahead. Bad habit of his. He even did it on the highway. We couldn't hear Mom over the grumble of the rusted out tailpipe – from which we were also treated to the occasional gulp of exhaust – but we knew she'd be yelling at him to slow down, watch where he was going. He'd be telling her to calm down, we'd be fine. All of a sudden he had his head out the window along with pointing, and we ran right into a dry ditch and came to a fast stop. The dust caught up with us. Timmy and me put our heads on our knees and covered ourselves with our arms. I was already crunching sand and knew I'd be picking it out of my hair and nose for a week. Trying to keep your mouth shut but also trying to breathe through your clogged up nose is one of those rock-and-a-hard-place situations. You alternate between crunching or blowing your nose on your finger. Timmy used to love wiping his snot on me. He knew I hated that. I swear, little brothers.

We'd gone off the left side of the road and were sitting sideways. When Dad opened the door gravity took it and bashed it against on old pinon trunk. He laughed like crazy. We could hear Mom cussing at him as she slid across the seat and out the door on his side. Dad caught her on the way down. They hugged and laughed.

Me and Timmy bailed out over the side and came over to survey just how deep we were in. Mostly just the one front tire and not up past the hub. We'd seen worse, so we ran off into the brush to let the grownups do the digging and arguing. We scared up a couple of jackrabbits that went zigzagging like rockets away from us. The way they jump up out of nowhere gives you a jolt like a scary movie. The fun kind of scared.

Nevada kids are tuned for rattlesnakes. It's instinct. We totally don't think about listening for them. The most important time to remember to get a visual on them is in the first part of spring when it's still too cold for them to move very fast, and they don't have the strength to rattle but do have the reflex to bite if you're too close. They're looking for warms spots in the sunny sand after hibernating under the brush. You'd be walking along, minding your own business, and you'd nearly step on one of those suckers laying full length across your path. That kind of scared is a little too scary for anyone even if you know rattlesnakes have to coil to get a good strike. I don't like snakes. Not even the gartersnakes—he called them "gardener snakes"–Timmy brought home all the time. The idea of stepping on one and even just feeling it move is enough to give me the heeby-jeebies. I beat Timmy nearly to a pulp when he left a harmless little gartersnake in my bed. He never tried that again. Dad had to pull me off of him.

There we were that day. Lost but not too. We knew Dad would whistle us back when he was ready. We kept on exploring. When Timmy and me lost sight of one another, we'd yell "Marco" and "Polo" til we came back together. I liked to look for little flowers and pretty rocks. I wanted to find gold. There had to be some left out there somewhere, why shouldn't I be the one to find some treasure? Critters were Timmy's area, and as far as I was concerned he could have them all with their ticks and teeth and claws. I looked for what was staying still and hidden in shadows or barely sticking out of the sand. I looked for mysteries and stuff you just don't see every day — especially because you're not looking close enough. Most people ignore the small stuff. Miss out on the chance to discover something rare. I've found hunks of obsidian and quartz and granite covered in fool's gold and even some turquoise. Arrowheads and purple glass and rusty bridle parts and curled up leather. Shell casings, lots of those. Skulls and skeletons. A bent up license plate so rusted it had holes eaten in it. A No Trespassing sign blasted to hell by shotguns. The usual.

But this day the biggest find was Timmy's. And I do mean big. I Marco Poloed my way to him, and there he was staring at a towering heap of old wood and rusty metal. Though it was falling down in places, you could still see that it was mining equipment, just like the pictures at the Nevada State Museum.

Another handy fact Nevada kids know is that if you see an abandoned mine operation, there are going to be tunnels *everywhere*. No sure way to watch your step. Cave-ins and shafts open up all the time, and every year at least one person gets swallowed up. Still, exploring is too hard to resist.

A find like Timmy's might as well've been actual gold. We ran to it and started crawling through its innards and up its supports. Mines had been all over the place during the days of the Comstock Lode. I never thought I'd see one this big in person, and of course I was hoping to find gold or silver, but just being here was a dream come true.

Lizards scattered away from us. I didn't even want to think about the scorpions and black widows. I grabbed a stick and tapped it in front of me to clear them out. If there were snakes, I didn't see them. No great loss.

Pretty soon we heard Dad whistle, but instead of going back, we called him to us. They came tramping over the tumbleweeds and sagebrush. They looked as astonished as we had. Dad, who knew his mining history, told us he thought this was part of the Douglas claim from back in the 1890s. There wasn't much silver left to find by then, and getting to it was harder and harder to do. Busting it out of other rocks was what this contraption was built for.

Wood in the desert weathers fast into splinters and crevasses. The soft part of the wood shrinks down and the harder part pokes up in lines that look like rows of razorblades. The soft parts turn gray and the hard parts turn orangish brown for a while before the whole thing turns solid gray. The splinters are humongous and hurt like hell. It's pretty hard to avoid them when you go picking through a pile. We had a great time exploring the wreckage anyway. We had Bactine and tweezers back at the truck. We'd be fine.

That was a fun day, a great day. The four of us prowled around until it started to get dark. Even the sunset was fantastic. Timmy and I talked non-stop all the way back to town, we were so excited. And we made a pact that we wouldn't tell anybody what we had seen. No sense it making our discovery into a tourist attraction. It would be ours and stay ours. When we got home we told the folks what we decided, and they agreed to keep the secret, too. We swore an oath on a stack of National Geographics just like always. We were a family who knew how to keep secrets. Turns out that it's a good skill to have if you're in the business of making people give up theirs.

💧

Ah, the good old days. Hadn't thought about that mine in years.

I blow smoke up toward intensely blue sky that looks close enough to touch. God, Flack, how you do get romantic when you get outdoors. I raise up on one elbow, unscrew the top on my ever-handy bottle of Jim Beam, and take a leisurely swallow. Makes me shiver like the first one of the day always does. I ought to quit this drinking. Quit the cancer-sticks, too. With everybody from hippies to straights going on and on about getting healthy, eating ginseng and tofu and drinking carrot juice, smoking pot instead of swigging booze or smoking tobacco, I feel very un-hip for being attached to my old-time chemicals. Poisoning myself into peace instead of seeking a squeaky-clean Nirvana. I tried pot a couple of times. Made me think about too much too hard for too long. That, I see, is the problem with this health nut craze: clarity. Who needs it? I like my world fuzzy around the edges. Some days, the fuzzier the better.

One more sip and I screw the top on and lie back. I'm heading down to Reno soon. Hardly businesslike to keep laying here, blowing smoke at the sky on a weekday morning. Especially when Johnny's out there on a rampage. . .

I sit up with a start. Mona. Shit, Mona! I took a couple of shots at her old man last night. He couldn't have gone merrily home to cocktails and dinner. And if he did go home, he couldn't have gone with a very good opinion of Mona's choice in friends. Or of Mona. I get to my feet. Put my cigarette out—for sure out, grew-up-in-the-desert out—on the sole of my boot, and grind the butt into shreds of paper and tobacco between my fingers, let the shreds scatter on the wet part of the sandy floor of the canyon. Rockalee is a few yards up from me and completely absorbed with the abundant fresh food that she's extra easy to catch. I lead her back to the steep part of the mountainside and climb onto the saddle. Got to get back to work. Time to check up on an old friend. And figure out what makes a new one tick.

Chapter 16

Red and Edie's oldest boy was Clyde. A twin to a sister named Clovis. Named for Edie's maternal great-grandparents. I guess if you get stuck with a name people kid you about all the time, you start to resent both the name and the people who gave it to you. Clyde was a bully to everybody. Just a mean hard-ass and, at seventeen, almost as physically big and powerful as Red. Clovis was a big girl like her brother but she handled whatever resentments she carried around by clamming up and learning to walk softly. She'd pass by you like you weren't there. Spent most of her time on her bed, reading steamy romances from the used bookstore. Red, that towering sweetheart of a man, was as different from his physically aggressive son as any two people could be.

The younger Larson kids and my little brother learned to stay out of Clyde's way at all costs. One of them was always on the look-out while the others played. Only the baby, three year old Bruce, seemed to soften up Clyde. He carried Bruce around, tickled him, talked to him. The rest of us – including his folks – just steered the hell clear of Clyde.

And I never did want to mention it. That in that house full of snores at night, Clyde found a real handy outlet for his bad attitude. I could count on it especially after he'd had a fight

146

with Red or Edie. The pig. Really got off on calling me names – whore, slut, bitch – while he held me by the hair and pumped himself into my mouth. Or. . .

I loved Red and Edie, and I understood that two more kids added to the pile they already had couldn't have been a picnic for them. It was a damn fine thing they did, making sure we didn't wind up separated into foster homes. I kept Clyde's fun and games to myself and swore to go on keeping quiet four more years until I finished high school and could get a job to take care of Timmy by myself. Putting up with Clyde now and then didn't seem like too outrageous a price for me to pay for our room and board. It wasn't. It wasn't.

But I don't know how we didn't hear the phone ring in the early hours of one morning. Or Red coming up the stairs to get me to go along with him to an investigation. No one in the house had had the slightest idea what Clyde was up to with me for two full years and I was proud of that. Then that early morning, Red was just there all of a sudden, throwing Clyde across the room, breaking the closet door. Vivvy and Beth whose room I shared stirred to life and started screaming as their father beat and beat and beat his oldest boy. It took all of us kids and Edie to get Red to stop but by the time we did, Clyde was unconscious. Eighteen hours later in intensive care, he died.

Edie became a whole new person. I'd seen this before with Mom: a massive, psychic overhaul. But where Mom had quickly withered and disintegrated, Edie blew up as big as an evil Thanksgiving Day parade balloon character. She blamed me for everything. Said I seduced her boy and said since I did that, I'd probably seduced her husband, too. When the court sentenced Red to twenty years for manslaughter, Edie said nothing to defend him. Didn't even cry. And that same day, she threw Timmy and me out. Said she didn't care what happened to us scheming bastards, home wreckers, just go. By the next month, she had sold everything and moved her family back to Tennessee. She didn't want to hear anything from me. Especially not "I'm sorry."

Chapter 17

Back at the stables I gave Rockalee a quick brushing. Got some of the Sawdust Trail off of her anyway. And what did I get for a thank you? As soon as I turned her loose in the corral, she flopped on her back and rolled around on purpose. Just to piss me off. She got up and shook out a cloud of dust that made her sneeze. Serves her right.

I don't notice how much of the Sawdust Trail and Rocky's hair I'm covered in until I jump into the GTO and raise a cloud of my own. Shit! Another fine mess. Can't worry about it now. Bigger fish to fry. I keep extra duds at the office for just this kind of situation. Horse hair's awful itchy.

Reno's growing too fast, becoming too citified. By 1980 it'll just be another Sacramento. I know it doesn't sound like an irritation depending on where you're from, but when you've grown up used to walking wherever or shooting cans wherever or parking wherever, hell, living wherever, all the new strip malls and apartments and McDonald's and subdivisions full of ticky-tack shacks don't seem like progress. I feel my Nevada getting buried under a lot of cheap plastic bullshit that only exists to make a handful of people a whole lot of money. Mark my words: it's where we're headed. And it's crowded and ugly. Maybe Montana . . .

It takes me a full fifteen minutes of circling to find a decent parking place, thinking I'd be saving time by paying a goddam meter closer to my office. Fifteen minutes of hide-and-seek is a new record for me. Downtown's packed. Every do-gooder civic organization in Reno must be holding a luncheon today from the looks of all the blue suits and high heels parading the sidewalks. Sure ain't tourists. Tourists only look this good at the dinner show in the Headliner Room.

I keep thinking someday I should get around to joining Rotary or one of those other clubs that let women in. Supposedly good for business. I'd want some nice little group that doesn't meet too often. Maybe does stuff for kids. Anything but Toastmasters. I don't know who's crazier in that bunch: the people wanting to stand up and blab or the people willing to listen to them. I probably wouldn't be too good at making deals and small talk over plates of warm rubber chicken anyway. Probably tell the wrong joke. The one about the guy who walks into a bar with a ten-inch pianist . . . You know the one.

My current pang of conscience toward community and fellow man lasts about three seconds—up until some model citizen flips me off for blocking a lane of Center Street traffic while parallel parking in a tight spot. I have the last laugh when he gets stuck behind another guy trying to do the same thing not even a block away.

If I was a better friend my fist order of business would be to check on Mona, but, hey, she's a big girl. King-Hi Jewelry and Loan is absolutely top priority. I have the winning ticket in my hip pocket, close to my heart. King-Hi's zillion flashing lights are blazing in the middle of the day during the energy crisis the news guys say we're all supposed to be freaked out over. The thing that hit me hard about this oil embargo bru-ha-ha is that for only the second time in my entire life I've seen casinos turn out their lights—which they have never done for any reason, even daylight. Now they're being asked to turn off the sparkles in the daytime. The only other occasion I remember seeing casinos go dark was the day Kennedy was shot: dark *and* closed casinos on that one terrible day. Anyway, King-Hi, like most of downtown, is thumbing its nose at Nixon and the energy crunch and Saudi Arabia just like good Nevadans should. In broad daylight.

I swing open the door to the pawn shop and an obnoxious buzzer announces me. A skinny old guy behind the counter looks up over his glasses and has to turn his head slightly to see past the assortment of tiny magnifying lenses attached to one side of his specs. He nods and goes back to examining the power tools a long-haired man in a plaid shirt with the sleeves cut out is offering to the altar of quick money and hoping to God to get back someday. I wander around and check out the gallery of guitars and watches and shotguns and wedding rings that will never see their rightful owners again. These places depress me. I can never go in one thinking "what a bargain." I'm always wondering why people need money so bad they'd sell their wedding rings. Or their tools or musical instruments. I wonder how much they miss what they've given up. How they felt when the final repayment date was coming around and there was no way they could get their stuff back. I wonder how it feels to see part of your life up for sale in a sleazy place like this.

The old guy behind the counter and the guy selling his tools reach their agreement. Or rather, the man with the tools accepts what he can get. They settle up the paperwork and cash money changes hands. The man who's sold his living opens his wallet and puts the wad of bills inside. He gives me a sad smile as he leaves.

"What can I do you for, dear?" The man behind the counter climbs down from a chrome barstool with a red pillow on the seat and becomes instantly shorter. He has a long-limbed, slender build that should have made him as tall as I thought he was. I know now that all of his height is from the waist up. He's wearing a brown string tie with a chunk of turquoise cinched up to his crepe-y throat. Needs a shave. Needs to quit smoking – his face has more cracks than a broken windshield, and I shudder to think that's how I'll look someday.

"Well, sweetie," I say, "I want to pick this up." I hold out the ticket. He takes it, climbs back up on his perch and swivels around to look up the number in his file. He pulls out a pink sheet of paper.

"Ruggerio." He takes his glasses off to get a real good look at me and says with a sneer, "You're a Ruggerio?"

"Hey, I'm holding the ticket, aren't I? That's what matters, isn't it? Says on the sign right behind you. Doesn't say a thing about needing a pedigree."

"Should have heard what the man with the pedigree said about my sign last night."

"When was this?"

"Right around closing. Midnight. Came in giving me all kinds of hell. But policy's policy. No tickee, no claimee."

"And he left?"

"This," he slams a short-stocked, pump shotgun down hard on the counter, "and the button I got here that rings straight to the cops were all the good-byes he needed."

Balls of steel on this man. Or maybe it's just that I know Johnny better than he does.

"Well, there's the tickee," I say.

"Yep."

"So?"

"You ain't from around here, are you, miss?"

152

"What makes you say that?"

"You don't seem to know who you're dealing with."

"Tell me your name then."

"Not me, dear. The individual whose ticket you're holding."

"Ruggerio, Johnny. About five-nine. Black hair. We met."

"And he gave you this?"

"Not exactly. It landed on my doorstep. Flack Murrow. Third floor." I hand him one of my cards. Time to get to know the neighbors.

"Yeah. 'Investigations,'" he reads and smirks. "I noticed your sign on the window up there. Thought you was a guy."

"Happens."

"How's business?"

"Getting there. I only opened a couple of months ago."

"Ernie. Ernie Marz. Assistant manager." He gives me a card. We shake hands. "Welcome to the neighborhood."

"Thanks. Hey, Ern, what about it?"

He spreads his hands. "What can I say? You got the ticket."

He leaves the claim check on the counter, puts his glasses on, and takes the pink sheet with him through a half-door to the back. A man about the size of my horse comes out from the doorway Ernie went through, wiping mayonnaise off the corners of his mustache. He's chewing a wad of food too big for his mouth and big enough for me to see. I decide to spend my time looking elsewhere. I remove the ticket from the counter and pretend to be interested in a display case full of diamonds.

Doesn't take Ernie long to find what he's looking for. The thing's only been in hock for six days. He comes through the doorway lugging a black rectangular gizmo with an eye piece on the side.

"Camera?" I ask. "Movie camera?"

"Sort of. Our friend Johnny called it a 'bay-ta-max.' See there?" Ernie points to the silver letters spelling out "Betamax." He says, "Ruggerio Junior was real hot I should get the name right. Takes moving pictures but you use these."

He opens the side of the Betamax and hands me a black plastic cartridge like an 8-track only a little longer and wider. Genius that I am, I shake it first then look at the flip side where there are two white gears recessed into the plastic. I find two small buttons on one long side. These release a cover that exposes a length of film.

"Shit!" I say. "I blew it."

"I don't think so. Johnny opened it for me like you just done. Didn't seem to matter to him. Said it's like music tape. You can use it over and over. This thing's supposed to record pictures like a tape recorder does music."

"Cool." I pick up the machine and look through the viewer. Ernie hams around for me. The thing is heavy as hell. Takes both hands. I turn it around and check out the lens.

"Hmm," I say, "you see something new every day. Heavy sucker." I set it down on the counter. "How much he owe you to get it back?"

"I only gave him twenty-five. He griped but not much. Couldn't give him more; hell, I didn't even know what it is. Probably go the way of the hula hoop. He'd've got more if he'd brought the dealie that shows the movie after you record it. That combo, I would have been interested in having around. Screwed up part is that he came back for it last night with no ticket. Know what I say about no tickee. Well, he sure didn't like the sound of that. But my old pal Smith and Wesson and my panic button won. He hightailed it out of here, screaming about coming back to kill me. Regular shit."

"What's the total?" I have money from the fishnet stocking to pay for Johnny's stuff.

"It'll be fifty."

"Steep." I stand a curled-up hundred on the counter.

"Sign here. I'll get you your change."

For a second, I almost write "Gladys Newbury" but decide on my regular name just in case Johnny turns up here again and wants to know where his "bay-ta-max" is. If it meant enough to him to take on this son of a bitch and his pump shotgun, he will probably want to see me about it soon. Might as well let him know exactly where it is.

"Here's your change, Miss Murrow. Or are you one of them libbers likes to be called 'Mzzz?'"

"Actually, I think Flack is fine between us, Ern. Thanks for your help. If Johnny comes by, go ahead and let him know where he can find this."

"You sure? He was a wild sum'bitch in here last night."

"Like I said before, we've met. He was wild then, too."

"Okay, hon, you're the boss."

"Right, toots. See you around."

Men and their "honeys" and "dears" and "sweeties." I don't consider myself a libber even though I'm indebted to them for what they did for the cause of bralessness. Gone without one since I was twenty-two and only go back on special occasions. But this honey/sweetie thing . . . Every man who calls me "sweetie-pie" gets a "toots" in return. Like to see more women catch onto the idea. The men we women deal with need to get hip that we're not all their girlfriends or their daughters. Most men don't notice when I serve them back their own medicine. They're too busy talking down to anything with tits to notice they've been toots-ed. But *I* know I toots-ed them, and it does give me some satisfaction.

I leave through the growling buzzer, make an immediate right on the sidewalk, and go through the entry to my part of the building. I see that Felix has had someone — he would never get his own hands dirty — take away the broken banister and nail up what I hope is only a temporary railing made of naked two by fours. I trudge up the three flights, lugging the ten ton Betamax, and I'm relieved to find Mona and Pioche sitting safe and sound on the ratty carpet outside my office.

"Afternoon, ladies," I say.

They both jump—not expecting me?—and before she has a chance to pull herself together, Mona looks like she has no more wheels left to spin. Then she plasters on that Jackie K charm quick as a wink. Pioche is propped up against Mona's knees and goes back to pulling at her mom's lips.

"Been here long?" I ask, putting the Betamax down by the door so I can get my keys out.

"What's this?"

"New toy. Got it at K-Mart. On sale."

"Bullshit." I wonder if that's what the Lady Jackie says under pressure. While I'm cussing at the lock that I blame for getting me into all of this in the first place, Mona gets up from the dirty carpet and gathers up her purse and her baby's belongings which appear to be more than are required to change a diaper. I coax the door into opening finally and let the ladies in, then retrieve the Betamax and follow them inside.

"Competition time for the Good Housekeeping Seal of Approval?" Mona's looking at the disaster the two goons and the police made of my office. Now there's black fingerprint dust on everything to go along with the mess of papers and overturned chairs.

"Had a little trouble, as you know. Here, I'll get you a chair."

Pioche starts to cry. Babies are more sensitive than we give them credit for; she can tell something ain't right. Mona tries to calm her down, but Pioche is smart enough to keep crying. I might cry, too, if I had any sense.

I wipe as much black powder as I can off one of my better chairs. Mona is pacing, bouncing Pioche, and shushing at her.

I lay my bag on the desk by the camera. Pioche hears the noise of all those glass beads clacking together and focuses her attention on this less hostile feature of her environment. I take the bag over to her and shake the leather fringe, making the beads rattle. Her little fingers reach out for a handful that goes directly into her mouth.

"Susan Anne, that is disgusting," says Mona, trying to get the fringe away from her baby. Pioche starts crying again.

"It's not going to kill her. Look, she's happy." The baby has a big mouthful of leather and beads, and Mona's too tired to argue. She plops down on the chair with the baby on her lap. Pioche sucks away on the yummy cowhide.

"If you'll excuse me, I need to get out of these jeans," I say. Suddenly, I'm not sure I can convince myself to sit down on the chair that was a throne for a stiff just yesterday. And there's also the thing of the chair being covered with black dust. I decide to kick my boots off standing up. Take off my jeans and use them to wipe down the chair. Toss them over by the bookcase. My other pants are in the bottom right desk drawer. Bonus: there are clean undies, too. I toss the pair I'm wearing onto the hairy Levi's.

"If you've finished your little peep show, do you suppose you could tell me about the video camera?"

"Video?"

"That's what it is. A video camera."

"What would you know about it?"

"I have one like it."

"Is that right? Show me how it works."

"Some other time if you don't mind. Where did you get this one?"

"Okay. Whole story: I found a claim check on Michael, your pal, before he met his maker in this very chair. Had to see what it was for. I just got this thing out of hock downstairs."

"That bastard."

"Michael?"

"No. Johnny."

"Yeah, the claim check was in his name."

"That unmitigated shit."

"Whoa, lady, your past is showing. What's the deal with this thing?"

"It's mine."

"Yours? Never figured you'd be into gadgets, Mo."

"And you'd be correct. However, if one wishes to obtain a visual record of certain . . . proceedings . . . without the knowledge of even a photo lab technician, this is the perfect item."

"Is that right? What kind of 'proceedings' might one want to record with this?" See? I can do Jackie K, too.

"First, there is the obvious: sex. Johnny gave the camera to me, and we made little inspirational tapes of our intimate moments."

"You did?"

"Of course, darling. What does it hurt? And when one grows tired of viewing a certain tape, one simply records a new episode over it."

"Expensive?"

"Very."

"I sure never saw one before."

"Not many people have."

I pick up the camera with new respect. Maybe it won't be just a fad like Ernie thinks. Mona's starting to make it sound like fun.

"So, no processing or anything?"

"None. The picture and sound . . ."

"Sound too?"

"Yes, sound. The picture and sound are instantly recorded and can be played back immediately if you wish or stored indefinitely."

"Far out. Too bad the thing weighs a ton. They've got those home movie jobs down to a some sort of reasonable size."

"The weight is a problem. A tripod is helpful especially when one's . . . hands are not free."

"Kinky."

"Correct."

"Man, this could revolutionize my business." I aim the camera at the Cal Neva. "I could catch people in the act, moving and talking, and show my client the cold facts on tape rather than a pile of photos and a transcript. But what plays it?"

"The device is like an 8-track deck only much larger. It hooks up to your television."

"Well, I'll be damned. I'm going to get one of these as soon as business picks up."

"As it is bound to."

"Thanks. Now, why would Johnny hock this valuable and entertaining item? The dude at King-Hi only gave him twenty-five bucks."

"Surely you realize it wasn't for the money. He obviously intended to hide the camera from me."

"Thought you two enjoyed your toy."

"Yes. And we also discovered it had many other uses. Johnny was first to employ the hidden camera technique. He taped me in the tub. Outside on the grounds. He came to delight in leaving it running somewhere out of sight to see what went on in different parts of the house when we didn't know we were being watched. Soon, we all knew we could be watched anywhere at any time. Then one day he made a recording of Michael and me as we were talking in the game room. It was a private matter . . ."

I give her the raised eyebrow.

"Not what you think. Not what Johnny thought, either. May I continue?"

"I'm all ears."

"No. You, my dear, are all hair. Well, without going into detail, we spoke in a sort of code we'd developed, knowing that Johnny's little spy could be lurking in the shadows. Your name, for example, never came up."

"*My* name?"

"I'll get to that in a moment."

"You damn well better."

"Flack, please . . . As you may well assume, Johnny thought he had caught Michael and me planning something altogether different. He called us into the living room and played the tape. It was horrible to feel so exposed. Horrible to watch and pray nothing hazardous would be revealed. Johnny and Michael had a terrible fight. I couldn't have planned it better if I'd tried."

"You planned for them to get into a fight?"

"At some point, yes. But not just then and not about Michael and me. Michael had been drinking heavily that night. His fatal flaw, as it were. He loved the stuff but had no constitution for it. He began raving about what a devious prick Johnny was and how Johnny'd better stay out of his private life or else. Bringing up his private life, of course, only made things worse. Johnny considered Michael his closest friend and what Johnny thought he had seen us doing called their whole relationship into question. No secrets among bosom buddies, as it were."

"I thought you said they were business partners."

"Oh yes. They are. But they met at college. Dorm mates: Michael, the promising scholarship student at B-school – business school – and Johnny, shipped off by his parents to avoid prosecution and scandal because of a land scam he'd cooked up. The senior Ruggerios bought baby boy a stellar high school transcript and college entrance exam scores and packed him off to Stanford which was, incidentally, close enough for them to keep a watchful eye on him."

"But he met up with Michael?"

"I think it was more the other way around in terms of who led whom into a life of crime. As I said, Michael was a scholarship student. From B.F.E., Nebraska. A bumpkin with frayed cuffs on his Sears button-downs but with business brains to spare. Johnny had more ideas and more money than practical sense. The two of them made a perfect partnership: Michael kept Johnny from losing his cool and going off the deep end, and Johnny supplied Michael with real-world capital and opportunities and grooming. At school, they ran liquor, drugs, girls, gambling—especially gambling—and made a fortune and a great many friends among the students and the more adventurous of the faculty members. However, once the administration caught on, Michael and Johnny were expelled. Stanford had to protect its reputation regardless of the Ruggerios dollars.

"Michael and Johnny decided Nevada would best befit their big money and big plans. Johnny had deep connections, and Michael loved dealing with the business affairs that bored Johnny senseless. Johnny got busy 'designing and building' the house we're living in. Once that was sufficiently underway, he and Michael started plotting and scheming with a vengeance. He transformed Michael into a well-dressed force to be reckoned with. And Michael loved that role. He would never have jeopardized his situation with Johnny. If it hadn't been for me."

"Oh my."

"I needed his skills, too. But I didn't tell him I needed to use them against Johnny. I was sounding him out on hypotheticals as often as I could to see if I could turn him."

"Could you? Did you?"

"Nearly. As well you know."

"Right."

"Johnny gets ideas in his head. About what he sees or what he thinks he overhears. He doesn't ask for explanations. He never assumes or admits he's wrong. He just . . . acts. No one ever knows who's going to be next on his shit list."

"Mind my asking: how did our friend Johnny and you come about?"

She smiles. "It's horribly Cinderella, I almost hate to tell you."

"Go ahead. Make me gag."

Pioche is a mass of brown slobber from her cheeks to her belly button, but she keeps gnawing away at the fringe on my bag only pausing long enough to examine the next prospective mouthful before cramming it in. Mona's been forming curly topknots of her daughter's hair around her finger. Pioche is getting quite a 'do.

"Johnny and I met at one of his parent's parties," she says.

"You party with the Ruggerios?"

"Unbeknownst to me at the time, Johnny had arranged my invitation. His family's main broker is also my broker, and he had seen me in the office one day and decided he simply had to meet me. I'd have been crazy to turn it down."

"Aw, adorable."

"Hardly, my dear. It was golden. Of course I was three months pregnant at the time . . ."

"Bet that went over big."

"I had to work fast but by the time I had really begun to show, Johnny wouldn't let me leave his side though he made it clear that he wanted nothing to do with the baby."

"What about this kid's dad, if you don't mind me asking?"

"Oh God, must we?"

"Your call."

"Not now if you don't mind. To continue: I considered his lack of interest in Pioche equivalent to my calculated interest in him. A fair trade, although my end necessitated quite a bit more pretense. Wasn't the first time I'd done as much with a man, I assure you."

Mona shakes her head. "All the money the Ruggerios possess will never buy Johnny any moderation when it comes to love nor any taste when it comes to art. Look what he does: he could buy a thousand Betamaxes and yet he lets a sentimental attachment to me lead him in this ridiculous game of hiding rather than disposing of my camera simply because it's mine."

I say, "Go figure. So, you got Johnny-boy ga-ga over you and your eyes light up like a jackpot." I take a cigarette out of the pack on my desk and put my stocking feet up.

Mona continues, "To try to make this excessively long story somewhat shorter, Johnny's eavesdropping gave me an idea: why not turn the camera on him? I set the thing discreetly outside his office window one day when five men you would recognize from the newspapers were over to discuss the zoning for the racetrack. Oh, you probably don't know that Johnny is scheming to build a horse racing facility in Washoe Valley."

"Hon, a little birdy told me."

"What? Nothing's been made public yet."

"I try not to deal too much with the public."

"Shit. May I have one of those cigarettes, please?"

"Thought you quit."

"I have. And I will again."

I light Mona a Lucky and take it over to her. She's careful to keep the smoke away from Pioche who is trying to grab this new wonder.

"At any rate, I set up the camera and recorded their little meeting until the tape ran out. I have it here with me. It's quite . . . damning."

"The good ole boys getting together to decide the fate of the world without the world's consent, huh?"

"Precisely."

I'm getting lost in all of this. "Let's back up a couple of steps, okay? I ain't got as good a head for all this detail as you do."

"As you wish."

"Okay, first off, when was this big fight between Johnny and Michael and what happened?"

"Oh, I did skip over that rather quickly. The reason I brought it up was that, interestingly, it happened the night he came to visit you."

"Yeah, I'd say that's interesting. To me anyway."

"I apologize. I got ahead of myself. Michael stormed out of the house threatening Johnny and me and everyone else. But before he left, he must have taken some souvenirs because when Johnny discovered some of his things were missing, he went into a rage of his own. I must tell you, Flack, I was frightened. Truly, and you know I've been through my share of frightening situations."

"You brought them on yourself, Mo."

Mona starts looking around her for an ashtray. I reach across the desk and take the cigarette from her.

"Thank you," she says.

"Hey, that was a lousy thing for me to say, Mona. I'm sorry."

"It's alright. It's true."

"Yes, it is. Okay, Michael takes off mad and drunk, Johnny throws a tantrum—then what?"

"I tried to talk to Johnny. Calm him down. But he was furious. Finally, he storms out and leaves in his car. This, too, looks like an opportunity for me. You see, I had been trying to squeeze Michael out. Not that I have his head for business. I merely wanted to solidify my position at Johnny's side. I was using every means I could think of to convince Johnny that I could be more useful to him—in more ways—than Michael could ever be."

"I can just bet what 'means' you used."

"One uses what one has." And Mona does have nice ones—not that I lean that way or anything.

"Answer me this then, old buddy, why exactly was Michael following me? He kept quite a beefy dossier, you know. Looked important."

"It was a rouse."

"Rouse. Good word."

"I had to keep him occupied so I could work on Johnny. When I tried to think of a distraction—which included someone who could take care of herself and didn't scare easily—I thought of you."

"Is that supposed to be a compliment?"

"No. It ought to be an apology. I used you. I told them each a slightly different version of a story in which you were alleged to have something juicy on the Ruggerio family which might pay off handsomely if they watched and waited until the time was right."

"Whatever I was supposed to know they each thought was going to make them rich?"

"With your casino associations, you can see why such a story would hold its credibility."

"Sure, fine. Glad I could be of service."

"Again, I apologize. May I continue? Next, as I had not predicted, Johnny, ever impatient, took it upon himself to suggest that Michael stay close to you. See where you went. Who you saw, etcetera. And Michael, as I could have predicted, leapt at the chance to play I Spy. By that time, they were becoming suspicious of each other—something I wanted to happen—but also were coming too close to you—which I warned them could make you run—I tried to keep them away,

Susan Anne. But they wouldn't listen. Then poor Michael's time ran out just before he could discover that what you had was . . ."

"Nothing."

"Nothing that kept him quite busy, and nothing that would have been disastrous for me had you two spoken."

She takes a deep breath. "I think when he finally revealed himself to you, such as it was, it was more about hurting Johnny than about finding out what I said you knew. He was very drunk, irrational, off to a good start at screwing up that night."

"The man was falling down."

"Booze always got the best of him."

I squirm in the dead guy's chair and say, "Works out nice for you to have Michael out of the picture then, doesn't it?"

"Susan Anne, I did not kill Michael, nor did I arrange to have him killed, since that's what you're thinking. It wouldn't have been necessary and certainly not the kind of mess I want to contend with on top of everything else. And Johnny . . . He's been utterly heartbroken."

"Sure has a funny way of showing it."

"You don't know him as I do."

"Yeech. Don't remind me." The picture of the two of them seeing me off yesterday afternoon—Johnny with his hand on her crotch—springs into my mind like an obnoxious song.

"Who killed him then?" I ask.

"That's the problem. I don't know. Neither does Johnny. I mean, not exactly. But to both of us it looks as if Michael's death were intended more as a message than a murder."

"Huh?"

"Johnny's been stepping on some high-powered toes of late. People he needs on his side but whom he is too hot-headed to handle with the proper kid gloves. He's even crossed some of his parents' cronies."

"Bummer move."

"Yes, the possibilities of who may have sent this message, while not endless, are numerous." She shifts in her chair to cradle her yawning baby.

"Hand me a bottle out of that bag, please?"

"Sure thing." I dig out a bottle of what looks like apple juice.

"No," she says, "the one with milk in it, if you would."

"Sorry." I hand her the right one. Mona puts the nipple in Pioche's mouth and sways her body from side to side to rock the baby to sleep.

"The horse syringe," I say. "'Hands off this race track thing?' Am I getting it?"

"Doesn't it make sense?"

"I guess so."

"Recently, he's been terribly paranoid. It's his own fault, of course, but aren't most of one's problems of one's own making? That might explain why he hocked the Betamax. Safekeeping, as it were, until this all blows over. Or . . ."

"Or?"

". . . and it's a horrible thought: he's onto me. Knows I turned the tables and employed his little trick against him."

"Big oops."

"The tape I made in his office that day? It's worth millions—serious money from people who should never have been in the same room together."

"Mona, what have I told you time and time again about crime?"

"It doesn't pay. And you have always been wrong about that especially this time."

I wipe my hand over my face like Harney did when I was telling him the story of my life last night, and I cuss a string of my favorites.

"I meant it when I told you this was it. The last time for me. One last score. But now . . . With things the way they are around Johnny's . . ."

"Speaking of him, did you see your lover boy—or whatever he is—last night?"

"No, as a matter of fact. It was the first night we've spent apart. There was no call. No note. I found it odd, but I'll admit I valued the time his absence afforded me to think. I counted my blessings more than I worried, I'm ashamed to say."

"Well, I did see him. Saw him waste a couple of guys behind Landrums."

"Johnny? Are you sure?"

"I took a look right at him down the barrel of a .357. Got two shots off. Missed."

She doesn't look as startled as any normal person might about Johnny committing murder or about me shooting at him and just comments on my marksmanship, "Practice, practice, my dear."

"Well, I hit his car both times."

She's absorbing this information and I can practically hear the gears grinding in her brain.

"You like Johnny-boy, don't you? Just a little?"

Her face becomes a frozen mask that says everything. Or nothing.

I say, "I guess I can see the attraction in a weird way. He's got that june sayqua."

"Je ne sais qu'a."

"Whatever. What now, Mo?"

"I'll go ahead with my plans. Johnny and those men on the tape will all be happy to pay me what I want to keep their faces off the television news."

"I'm going to remind you that what you're planning is illegal as hell and I'm going to add potentially deadly."

"I realize that, but I'll take my chances.

"Then where do I come in in this bullshit where I don't belong, don't want to be, and resent you dragging me into?"

"All I want from you is that you take Pioche to San Francisco. I've made arrangements with a business acquaintance to have her flown to Hong Kong to stay with a nanny I've hired until I collect my money and can get away. Naturally, I will leave Johnny's before I let the players involved know what I have on them. As far as he will know from the hints I leave him, Pioche and I have simply disappeared underground together. I assume he will hire an army to come looking for us. I've planned for that. I will make it appear as though we're close by through the instructions he and his pals will receive about where and when to bring me my money."

"Where will you be then?"

"That's immaterial. All I care about is that my baby is safe — which is where you come in. I can work this deal more efficiently without having to worry about her. As you and I both know, I am perfectly capable of taking care of myself."

"God, Mo. I don't like this."

"Neither do I. It's for her, you see? Help me, and I swear I'll be a good girl from now on. Or, rather, from the day my deal is done."

I light two more cigarettes and take one to Mona.

"You want a drink?" I ask.

"Desperately."

I take the fifth of Beam, the aluminum tumbler, and a Cal Neva coffee cup out of my desk drawer. I let her have the tumbler because it's cleaner.

"To you, Mo. And to your beautiful daughter. Hope this works."

"So do I, my friend."

We clink, or rather clunk, our drinks.

She says, "More than anything, I want this baby girl to have a real home with me somewhere."

"When do you want me to take her to The City?"

"Tonight. Can you find your way back to Johnny's house?"

"Yeah."

"I'll see you at seven, then. I've taken the liberty of canceling the car he was sending for you at six."

I imagine the broken-hearted Duke spitting, "Good!" and stomping off to his cave to watch *That Girl.*

Mona says, "We'll tell Johnny you're taking her for the weekend because you're her auntie in a modern sense and you just love babies. I'll convince him to be delighted to have a weekend of my complete attention. I've brought some extra things for her now that I will leave here. That way when you come to get her tonight, it will look as if you are only taking enough for the weekend."

"Mona, I don't know dink about babies."

"Feed her when she's hungry. Change her when she's wet. Hold her. Talk to her. And let her chew on that ghastly bag of yours, I suppose. She seems to like it. Here's five thousand dollars. That should be sufficient for the trip."

"Keep your money, Mo. I'm flush."

She tosses the wad of bills on my desk. People are always throwing five thousand bucks at me these days. "Well, then," she says, "hire a decorator, for heaven's sake. And do something with your hair."

We laugh. Then she talks me point by point through a sheet of instructions about the where and when and who in San Francisco. I refill her tumbler and she tosses it down like a wrangler. Then they leave.

I take Pioche's gear and the video camera downstairs and put them into the trunk of my car alongside the saddle. Mona would probably hyperventilate if she saw all that pretty pink fluff next to the sweaty horse blanket. I put a couple of nickels into the meter and go upstairs to see if I can force myself to concentrate on work until it's time to leave for Johnny's.

Shit. You don't have to tell me I should've told Mona to forget it. And you don't have to remind me it's not written in blood that I have to show up at Johnny's tonight. What the hell do I owe her, anyway, the crook? Contributing to this deal she claims is her big finale is a total about-face for me: "Sure, Mo, it's okay to get money out of thieving bastards just because they are thieving bastards. We all know they deserve it. They can afford it. What goes around, comes around."

How come I'm not making plans to hide in the weeds, waiting to bust Mona for this thing she's about to do? Bust the no-goods on the videotape, too, while I'm at it. I should be chomping at the bit to get my hands on all of them for everything they've done or ever thought about doing. This is the best chance I've had to get her. Instead, I'm offering to *help* her. What ever happened to my golden rule where a crime's a crime – all things being first and finally exactly what they are?

Damn Mona just had to have a baby; the baby just had to be a cute little girl who needs my help and knows nothing about old associations, history, what I tried – and failed – to do to help my own brother. What I never meant to do to Red. Because I don't see an end to paying for all the trouble I've brought on people I love, I can't possibly say "leave me out of this" to Mona. This scam could buy her baby Beaver Cleaver's life. How can I feel except . . . I don't want to know too much about how I feel.

Except that it's damn distracting. I keep trying to concentrate on the mountain of work in front of me. Concentrate on being 28 years old instead of 14. Start to write something in a file or reach for the phone to call a client when I find myself staring at the dark stains from Pioche's fresh slobber on my bag and at the Betamax lens pointed straight at me. It's a done deal that I will keep my hands to myself while Mona masterminds this one last crime. I will do what she's asked.

Shit. Shit. Shit.

After I've dialed the wrong number twice in a row, I give in to the hopelessness of getting anything important done. I rock back in my squeaky swivel chair and watch the shadows of the afternoon sun cast the slanted, backwards letters of my name across the floor and part way up the side of the wall. Have another drink and smoke the last of my cigarettes. Oh darn, now I'll have to go out. And to make the trip downstairs worthwhile – and help me feel like I've accomplished something productive–I call Harney at the police station on my way out the door to tell him I'm coming by with Michael's stuff. It cheers him up to hear that I'm actually going to do what I said I'd do. And on the day I said I'd do it. And, of course, it gives me somewhere to be besides here.

Chapter 18

Red asked to see me on the day before he was to be transferred from the Washoe County Jail down to the state prison in Carson City. That last day, he talked to his own kids—the ones Edie hadn't managed to turn against him—and to Timmy. Then he asked to see me separately from the others which caused a big stir because everyone "knew" I was the reason Red was in jail. Susan Anne Murrow: brave, dead fireman's daughter. Teenage homewrecker. Seducer of grown men and their sons. But over Edie's loud objections that day, Red got this final favor from the long arm of the law who used to be his friends.

Timmy and I had been on our own for three months by the time they sentenced Red. He had to get someone to call a couple of the boys from the firehouse to go out looking for us. They found us at the Gospel Mission on Commercial Row where we were getting some breakfast before Timmy caught the school bus. We'd been doing okay, off and on. That day was one of those off times when we had to stand in line or go hungry. The closer we came to my payday, the more often we dined at the Mission. We'd make it quick. And make it look like we were with Bud and his schizophrenic girlfriend or one of the other down-and-outer couples. Some of the serving people behind the counter were beginning to recognize our faces, so every time we went down there it was a rush between us and our food and any can't-mind-their-own-business goodie-goodies hot to commit us to the state orphanage for our "protection." Tough to enjoy a meal under those circumstances—not that there was much to enjoy about the food in the first place. But all that starch and sugar was the manna from heaven that kept up Timmy's strength for school and me for my table bussing job at the Primadonna. The Gospel Mission. That's where they found us on Red's last day in Reno.

The Flack Murrow who Bobby and Fred presented to Red in the jail visiting room was looking and feeling about as weak as a half-drowned kitten, but I was still standing. Red's normally rosy face looked more gray than red. Exhausted. Confused by what happened to him, how fast it happened, and how Edie could turn on him in a heartbeat without mussing a hair on her head. He smiled when he saw me come in and tried to stand up—hands cuffed in front—but the two guards behind him put their hands on his shoulders and made him stay seated. That was when I lost it — started blubbering like a brat. Saying, "I'm sorry, I'm sorry, I'm sorry." Red was quiet while I cried it out. Sitting across the metal table from me, wiping away enough tears of his own, the chain between his hands clicking.

"Flack," he said once he could trust his mouth to make words, "you didn't do nothing wrong, you hear me? Christ, I didn't do nothing wrong. But here we are, the worst hurt among the living by what went on."

He ran a hand through his already messed up hair. "Funny how things change so fast," he said. "One day, you got a family around you and work you love doing and the next . . . Shit, you've been through it twice. Hit me last night: you lost two families."

He smiled a real weak smile and ran the back of his hand under his nose. Then he leaned toward me which made the guards move up behind him again.

"I'm the one who's sorry," he said and hung his head for a few minutes. "I let you down every way I can think of. Your dad . . . This . . . I'd do anything for you and your little brother, you know that? You're like two of my own. And I let you down."

He cried til his shoulders shook. I didn't have a Kleenex. I almost offered him a cigarette instead but realized I'd be handing him Edie's brand. I lit one for myself anyway. I wanted to say something to him. Digging around in the corners of my mind for something smart, for just the right something. And all I could come up with was:

"I'm scared, Red."

I immediately felt selfish for saying it. Here I was hoping to comfort him and all I was thinking about was myself.

One of the guards said our time was up and Red said, "I'm scared, too, youngster. Come and see me when you can, will you do that?"

"You know I will. Hey, Red?"

He was standing between the guards who held him by his upper arms.

"What, kitten?"

Pop used to call me that.

"I love you, Red.

"Thanks," he said and smiled just a little. "Someone'd better."

He nodded to me before the guards turned him and led him through the barred door. I knew that nod said he loved me, too.

I turned and went out the other door to freedom—whatever that was supposed to mean. Walked down the corridor still lined with Red's real family — Edie included, though she never spoke to him. Some were crying. Some drilling the darts of their eyes into me. At the end of the hall, Timmy sat alone on a wooden chair, scuffing his feet back and forth on the floor. He didn't notice me until I was directly in front of him. Then he stood up and walked ahead of me in silence through all the looks of all the people working in the jail that day. Grady was there. The only one who looked sad. Everyone knew about me. All about me, they thought. Funny how people will play parts just perfect—just like on a t.v. show. Nowhere in the script did it say to ask what really happened.

Chapter 19

Rodney opens the purple door for me at Johnny's. He's holding a baby bottle full of milk. A fluffy blanket with pink cows jumping over blue moons is draped over his shoulder. He's wearing an Afro-patterned caftan.

"'s hap'nin'?" he says, holding in a hit of the joint he's smoking and stepping aside for me.

"Not too much."

"Looking for Mona? She on the back deck. Go on through the living room. You'll see her."

"Thanks."

Rodney bops down the hall and into a room that's emitting spinning patterns of red, yellow, and blue star-shaped light onto the opposite wall. Over a soft chorus of "Everybody is a Star," I hear Pioche getting excited at the prospect of dinner and Rodney saying, "Be cool, sugar plum – it's coming right up." The door shuts and the hallway goes dark and abruptly silent.

I walk through the mood-lit living room, trying not to fall over – or knock over – any valuable pieces of art. Where are the eleven billion lights that were blazing over the bar yesterday now that I need them? I pick my way across the wide, obstacle-filled room, focused partly on the welfare of my toes and partly on trying to see, through the reflections in the glass wall on the opposite side, if Mona's alone in the dark. The arc of the lighted end of a cigarette shows me where a person is standing. It's not until I slide open the glass door that I can make out Mona's shape leaning against the railing. Dark piñons and junipers lurk behind her against the very last light of day. She's alone. She swings around at the sound of me opening the door, coiled like she might take off running.

"Little jumpy, are we?" I say.

"Susan Anne."

"Expecting someone else? Where's your sweetheart?"

"He hasn't returned."

"Would you, considering?"

"Did it ever occur to you that I might be worried?"

"Don't be. He'll turn up. You'll get your money."

"It's not necessary to be crass."

"But isn't that what you were thinking . . . first?"

Mona looks away from me.

"Kind of quiet around the old homestead tonight," I say. "Where is everybody?"

"I'm giving them a surprise—oh, shall we call it 'company party.' Sonny and Cher at the Lake. Limos. Dinner show. They think it's Johnny's treat."

"What about Rodney?"

"He's not much for socializing which works out just fine for tonight. Someone should witness you playing the happy auntie."

"Probably right. I'll say, though, that a dope-smoking cat like Rodney wouldn't strike me as my first choice for a baby-sitter. Is that his official title?"

"No. Bodyguard, officially."

"Who just happens to be good with babies?"

"Adores her, fortunately for both of them. Johnny 'assigned' Rodney to her. He's a blessing." Mona grinds her cigarette out thoroughly—Nevada style—in a metal ashtray. I start groping inside my bag for the pack of Luckies I can't seem to find. Mona holds out a box of Virginia Slims. I take one.

"Aren't these dainty. Not much flavor."

"Some people like flavors other than that shredded tree bark you smoke."

"There are worse things I could be doing."

"Name one."

"Give me a minute. I'll think of something."

The sliding door opens, and Mona and I both jump out of our skins. It's Rodney bringing the pajamaed and sweet-smelling Pioche to her mother for a good-night kiss. Mona goes into her act.

"Oh, Rodney, I'm sorry. I forgot to mention that Flack is taking Pioche for the weekend."

He looks at me suspiciously, tightening his arms around the baby though I don't think he notices he's doing it.

Rodney says, "Who she is, anyway, she can come out here and just take the baby?"

"We are very old friends. We've known each other since we were six or seven."

"Seven," I say.

"Yes," says Mona, "and as I am not on speaking terms with anyone in my immediate family, I think of Flack as the baby's adopted auntie."

Rodney's not liking this idea. He's recollecting that bit in the Holiday Inn parking lot which was not exactly a scene from *The Partridge Family*. He glares from Mona to me to Mona to me like he's watching us play pingpong. Mona walks over to him and holds out her arms for Pioche who starts wiggling her legs and straining toward her mom. Rodney eyeballs me as he passes the baby to Mona.

"What you know about taking care of a baby?" he asks, crossing his empty arms.

"Hey, I was a baby myself once. Nothing to it."

"Mona, I don't . . .," Rodney starts.

"I appreciate your concern but there's absolutely nothing to worry about. Here. See?" She hands the baby to me, and the expression on her face begs me not screw up. I take the kid under the arms then remember to hold her against my chest with my arms around her and go "goo goo ga ga." For some reason, Pioche loves it. Starts pumping her little legs and drooling. I do it some more. This is kind of fun.

"You see, Rodney? There's no cause for alarm."

"Bet she don't know how to feed her. Or when. Or how to change a diaper or when's bedtime or nothing. And what we going to say to Johnny? I got my orders."

Mona kisses Rodney on the cheek. "You're a sweetie," she coos. "I'll tell you what: since Flack and I would like a few minutes to talk about this weekend, why don't you put Pioche to bed for now and collect a few of her favorite things to send along? Will you do that for me, please?"

I pass the baby to Rodney. He looks relieved to be in charge again, but I can't think he's any closer to buying my qualifications. I don't blame him — he's definitely the expert. He gives me another disapproving once-over, opens the slider, and disappears into the dark house with the baby and without another word.

Mona says, "That should keep him occupied for a while. Would you care for a drink?"

"Yes, ma'am. Make mine a double bourbon. No water, no ice. Maybe just the bottle and no glass."

She rolls her eyes at me. "Barbarian."

"Bourbonian?"

Mona goes inside and leaves me alone on the deck to appreciate the deep peace she enjoys every night in her present surroundings. Up here, far from town, you can see a zillion stars. The wide, white band of the Milky Way glows like that shiny stuff that floats on the ocean. I forget what the heck it's called. At this point in early May, frog mating season is in full, erotic swing. You'd think, if you were inclined to think about frogs, that the ones I'm hearing would be big bruisers with legs like turkey drumsticks. But Nevada frogs are mostly itty-bitty, fingertip-size boogers. Which is probably why they're so loud: they're too small to find each other by sight over a huge space. Must be quite a few nice watering holes up this canyon, judging from the volume and variety of croaks. I'll get Rockalee up here someday, go for a snoop.

It's amazing how a loud, unexpected noise will shut down the ribbit of every frog for miles. They respond to the faint click of a car door being eased shut before it registers in my pea-brain. Suddenly there is not a sound except my heartbeat and someone running up the asphalt on the other side of the house. I back away from the railing, and head for the door, straining to see and hear through the thick darkness. The frogs who were slowly resuming their mating calls stop, too. I keep a lookout in front of me while fumbling for the door handle – which seems miraculously to be changing positions behind me. And now, just so things could be as difficult as possible, the few lights in the house that were on – not that they were helping anyway – abruptly go off. All of them. And it's real, real damn dark real fast. I hear a crash and a "Shit" coming from inside. Probably some precious objet d'art meeting its demise.

Okay, I tell myself, we're way out in the sticks. They probably have outages up here all the time. There's probably a generator that we can go kick start. Or maybe it comes on

181

automatically once it realizes Sierra Pacific's dropped the ball again. This is what I'm telling myself. But I have no reason to suspect I'm telling the truth.

I finally get hold of the door handle and slide it open as quietly as I can. "Mona?" I whisper. Nothing comes back. "Mo?" I drop to a crouch behind the protective level of the furniture.

"Over here," Mona whispers. "By the bar. Go around by the fireplace. There's broken glass everywhere."

I try to recall the layout of the room but bump into assorted household goods until I feel Mona's hand on my leg. And I find that the crash I heard was even worse than I thought. Mona didn't break some piece of art, she tripped and broke our drinks all over the tile floor in front of the bar. The smell of wasted alcohol is enough to make you cry.

"Where's Rodney?" I ask.

"I hope he's in the baby's room. Did you see anything out there?"

"Nope. Heard a car door closing. Somebody running."

"Johnny?"

"How should I know? And why'd he be sneaking around his own house?"

"Mona?" It's Rodney with a flashlight. He's whispering, too. Sudden darkness will do that to a person. He focuses the beam on us. We must look like quite a pair, blinking at the light, huddled together against the bar and surrounded by broken glass.

He takes the clue and squats next to me. "Fuck's going on?"

I say, "Don't know. You two stay here. I'm going out front."

"This is some bullshit, man," Rodney says out loud. He stands up and points the flashlight at the glass wall facing the deck . . . illuminating Johnny. Same red shirt, white pants. Looking tired but also something else. Something unreasonable

yet weirdly calm around the mouth and nose. He slides the
door open.

"Turn that fucking thing off," Johnny says in a vague tone
like he's asking us how was our day.

Rodney cuts the light. "Johnny," Rodney says. "Man,
what you doing?"

"Coming home," says the voice out of the night.
"What're you doing?"

"Standing here in the dark, man. Let's go check them
breakers, okay?"

I detect a change in Rodney's voice. It's gone deeper
now. And he's stretching out his words in a way I've done
myself to calm that dingbat Rockalee. There's not a hint of
emotion, just direction. Sounds like Rodney's talked Johnny
down from more than a couple of high ledges.

"Are you alone in the dark, Rodney?" The question is
sheer sarcasm. He's seen a strange car in his driveway.

"I'm here, Johnny," says Mona.

"Me too," I say, and Mona punches me in the thigh.

"Ah, another familiar voice. Flac-K." Emphasizing the
"k" again.

Rodney makes a move. "Come on, John. The ladies are
freaked. Let's get the lights back on."

"Stay put, for Christ's sake," Johnny says. "Mona, where
is everyone?"

She clears her throat. "It's a surprise, darling. You're
always saying we never spend time alone. I've been planning
this day for months."

"This day," he says with even more of an edge.

"Yes, and Susan Anne's here to take Pioche, isn't that
nice?" Mona's following Rodney's lead: keeping her voice
low, too. Seductive, but her words come out carefully.

"Just you and me. That's so, so nice," Johnny says.

"Tell you what," says Rodney. "Y'all stay here. I'll get the
lights."

Johnny says, "I said no, goddammit."

"Then what do you want to do?"

Johnny doesn't answer. Mona shifts her position next to me, sending some chunks of glass sliding over the tile.

"What's that?" Johnny asks.

Mona says, "I broke a couple of glasses when the lights went out. I'm sure it's a mess, but I can't see to clean it up."

"Oh, Mona wants the lights on."

"Yes, I would before someone gets hurt."

"Yeah. Wouldn't want anyone – possibly our guest – to get hurt. Yeah. Rodney, bring your light, and we'll go have a look at those breakers. For the ladies-s-s-s."

There he goes, reminding me of a snake again. Hissing out his words. Punctuating the hard sounds like a rattlesnake's rattle. The product of centuries of selective, dangerous breeding.

"I can turn this flashlight on now?" Rodney asks. "That okay?"

"Of course, of course."

Rodney switches on the beam, which comes to life then promptly dies. He hits it against his palm a few times to get it working. The weak light makes Johnny look like a vampire – granted, a very hip vampire with his mane of black hair and deep eyes. His skin color is completely washed out, seems to glow. Mona and I get up off the floor now that we can see to avoid being sliced and diced.

"Come here, babe," Johnny says.

I easily figure he doesn't mean me. He holds out a beckoning arm. A long second goes by before Mona can make herself move forward. Rodney takes her by the elbow. Mona and Rodney move away from me, and the light goes with them. Johnny gathers Mona around the waist with one arm and pulls her in. Kisses her for a romantic duration. If she feels to him as stiff as she looks to me, we could be in a world of trouble.

He says to her, "You're sweet. Do you know how sweet you are? Planning a surprise for me? It's just sweet. Sweet is what it is. I've missed you, honey."

"Oh Johnny, you've had me worried."

Geez, I'm thinking, which corny movie are we in?

He slides an elegant forefinger down the bridge of her nose.

"She's great," he says. "Isn't she great?"

Rodney and I mumble and grunt our agreement. Johnny kisses Mona again with plenty of smacks and slurps. I start to feel I should look the other way, but I don't. Mona's posture gives me the impression that this is not their usual level of mushiness in front of a crowd. She's just going along.

"Your man'll be right back, babe," he says.

Rodney slides the glass door part way open. He and Johnny both stand back to let the other guy go out first. Then they both try to go out at the same time. Rodney ends up putting a hand on Johnny's shoulder and guiding him out the door. Johnny walks on ahead while Rodney looks back into the house. I wish I could tell more from his expression as he closes the slider. Flashlight glow bounces off the sage and piñons in step with Rodney's bouncy stride as the men walk toward the left side of the deck and out of my vision.

"What do you want to do now?" I ask Mona. "Tell ghost stories? Where are my smokes? Oh shit! Be right back."

I nearly go into shock when I remember my bag with my .357 inside is still outside on the table where we had been smoking, where Rodney and Johnny just passed by. I open the door as carefully as I can, listening for the menfolks, before crawling over and grabbing my stuff. Oh man! That was a scary moment! I don't like being separated from my Python on a good day, and this situation?

"Okay," I say. "What can we do for light?"

"There are candles all over this room. By the fireplace. On the bar. Is your lighter handy?"

"Right here in my front pocket."

The little flame's not much help, but I can see a folk art candelabra-thingy on the coffee table. I get two of the eight candles lit before the metal overheats and burns my fingers. Been doing that a lot lately. I pass one of the candles to Mona, and she lights some thick white ones in tall brass holders on each side of the fireplace opening.

"Oh, this should help too . . ." she says. She bends down by the fireplace, and blue flames poof to life where logs ought to be, and the blue gets brighter and brighter until it's mostly yellow.

"Gas fireplace," I say. "Rich people do have all the good toys."

This side of the room is alive with long, creepy shadows. The rest of the place is pitch black. Mona finds a broom behind the bar, and we scoop up as much of the broken glass as we can see. By my calculations, the lights should be coming on any time, which is fine with me. What we have now is hardly creating a mood. Not under these circumstances. We scoop the forlorn, glittering scraps of our drinks into a garbage can behind the bar. Mona grabs a fresh bottle of something brown off the nearest shelf and hands it to me. I uncap it and drink with gratitude.

Mona sits down on the arm of the couch. "Johnny's acting very, very strangely," she says. Her eyebrows are all knotted in the middle like this is some big, exotic news flash.

"Glad to hear it," I say. "I thought it was just me."

"No. No. This is strange – even for him."

"Okay, the dude's strange. I don't know what other problems he has, but if – and it ain't a very big if – Johnny's responsible for cutting the power, why do you think he might do it?"

"Is this rhetorical?"

"Is it what?"

"Never mind. He'd cut the power to . . .?"

"Look, Mo, the man's swimming in death lately – all of it, in one way or another, connected to him. He finally makes his way home. It's too quiet. There's a strange car out front. He already knows he's ass-deep in trouble. Who's here? What do they want? What's up?"

"Yes, I see."

"Now, he cuts the lights to get a chance to scare the shit out of whoever's in his house and to buy time to decide what to do. Right now, he's got Rodney. I figure he's separating us from each other. One against two – especially if they're just chicks – is better than one against three, right?"

"Right."

"Even now Rodney's out there doing his job: taking care of the baby, you, the homestead. Almost seems innocent enough."

"And?"

"Now that Johnny's whittled down the opposition, what do you want to bet he comes back in alone?"

"Oh God," Mona says.

"Right."

Mona and I sit and listen to each other breathe for a few seconds, then I say, "You need to get Pioche to a safe place. Now."

"But I want you to . . ."

"I think maybe that ship sailed."

"Why?"

"I think you're in more danger than you think."

"Flack, I . . . I haven't exactly told you the whole reason I need you to take her."

"Do I really need to hear this?"

"I know that whatever Johnny's pissed about has to do with me. Not business. Not you. It's me."

"And?"

"And, if I can't pillow talk him out of it, things could get . . ."

187

"Then you need me. Let Rodney take the kid. He can take my car too if he needs it."

"No, this is on me. Whatever it is. I can handle him one way or the other if you get my drift. I can't risk her getting hurt."

"This is crazy."

"Darling, you don't know the half of it."

"You can catch me up on the details later, but for now, I'm not budging."

"Susan Anne, please."

I take a long pull on the jug of whatever it is she's handed me that I wish wasn't quite so sickening sweet but is doing the trick anyway.

I say, "*You* take her and go. Now. Leave this mess to the professionals."

She looks at me with those Liz Taylor eyes, those experienced, capable eyes, and flips me the bird. I take this opportunity to slap her. Hard enough to turn her head. Her mouth gapes open, and her beautifully manicured hand goes up to her cheek. We glare at each other for a long moment. Her hand goes down, her shoulders sag, and she lets a little tear fall down her lily-white cheek onto her lily-white breast.

She clears her throat and shakes her head to clear it, too.

"Where?" she asks.

"Here, my car keys. Do this: dump my car somewhere near my office, somewhere it won't get towed or stolen, preferably. Check into a room at the Mapes as Gladys Newbury. Stay there until I show up."

"How will you . . .?"

"Mona, shut up and go."

She leaves me and starts for Pioche's room then turns back.

"You're going to hate me . . ." she says.

I point down the hall like a pissed-off mom sending a brat to her room, then cross my arms over my chest. "Don't sweat it, Mo. I already hate you."

"No, listen. About Michael. I lied before. I . . ."

I put up my hands like I'm surrendering and say, "Not now, okay? Confession's not all that good for the soul."

Her face goes from beautiful to terrible all at once. Splotchy red in the face where I hit her and down her neck like she used to do when we were kids, and she had committed some nefarious act she had to cop to. Worried. Guilty. Scared. Mind not on her game.

"Mona," I yell to snap her out of it. "The baby." That gets her going again.

I know we're playing right into Johnny's hand by splitting up, but I also know I can only handle what's probably coming next if Pioche is safely out of the picture. Mona and I can go our separate ways. I hate to lose the advantage of her sneakiness and her spell over Johnny in the bargain, but I've been on my own in worse situations. The only thing to think about is the kid.

I take off and hang a right to go get familiar with this end of the house. I check the bathroom I've seen before. Open the door to the laundry room and listen inside. When I get to the end of the hall, it's a bit awkward opening that last door with a gun in one hand and a candle in the other. Once I'm inside, the candlelight glitters on the surface of a huge pool that looks like a bottomless pit at the moment. I sneak up a flight of stairs and find an impressive game room. Pool table, card table, full-on craps table, pinball machines, couple of slots. Weird to see it all dark. And so completely quiet. I don't like weird, you know. Also don't like being up a flight of stairs in a room that looks to have no other exit. The .357 leading the way, I go back down the stairs and out to the pool. I stop and listen. No pumps and slurps, only my heart beating loud in my ears. All of a sudden, hot wax drips onto the back of my hand and burns like hell.

"Shit," I say as I drop the candle. The flame sizzles and threatens to drown in melted wax on the floor. I go to shove the Python into the back of my waistband, miss, and it clatters to the concrete. All this time I'm blowing on my hand and cussing; neither one is doing any damn good.

I bend over quick to pick up the candle before it goes all the way out, then start feeling around for my gun, which, thank gawd, I find. But if that wasn't enough for one Nevada girl to juggle in one evening, a hand reaches out of the dark, covers my mouth and a stringy, strong arm pulls me up straight. I feel the point of a knife blade on my neck just under my left ear. Being trapped this way sort of seems like a rerun of a few days ago. One of those déja vus. But with a knife.

"Drop the gun, bitch," Johnny hisses against my neck.

I drop the Python as gently as I can onto the concrete again. Johnny kicks it across the floor, and I hear it dive into the pool. Oh, my poor baby!

With a hand over my mouth and the knife still at my throat, he escorts me back into the main hall. I feel a warm trickle of blood running from under my ear.

"Where's Mona?" He doesn't uncover my mouth, making me point with my forehead in the direction of Pioche's room. Johnny's hand smells like french fries.

"We'll wait here for your friend," he whispers as he moves us forward until we're blocking the entry door.

Mona comes out of Pioche's room butt-first, her arms full of the baby and the baby's stuff, trying to keep her candle from setting the whole works on fire. The baby is whimpering softly from being partially woken up. Mona staggers, hunched over, toward the front door.

"You can stop right there, lover," Johnny says out loud. "The gang's all here. Yeah. Put the brat back in her beddiebye. Us adults are going on into the living room and relax. Have a little chat."

Mona stops but does not turn around. She straightens her back and stands motionless, an overloaded statue. Johnny digs the knife in a little deeper into me. A new gush of blood runs down my shirt. I let out a little yelp I can't keep in.

"Goddammit, did you hear me?" he yells at Mona.

Mona doesn't say anything. Doesn't turn around. Just walks the baby back to her room. Shuts the door behind her when she comes out, empty hands clasped in front of her. She sees my predicament and struggles to keep the reaction off her face.

"Come here," he says to Mona. She comes a few steps closer, but she's still a good couple of yards away. "A little closer. A little closer. I won't bite. Yeah." Now he can reach her. He takes the knife away from my neck and grabs us both by the upper arms. "Get over on the fucking couch," Johnny says, pulling Mona and me into the orange glow of the living room. The blood seeping from my neck looks black where it has soaked one side of my shirt nearly to the waistband of my jeans. With Johnny propelling us, we work our way around to the front of the couch, and he sits us down. He steps up onto and over the table and crouches on the other side.

"That's going to leave a nasty scar," Johnny says, stabbing a leather-handled dagger into the wooden tabletop and leaning his chin on both hands on the hilt. He looks beyond tired and way beyond reason.

"Won't be the first," I say. I haven't touched it to see how bad it is, and I won't while he's watching.

"You think you're one tough motherfucking broad, don't you?"

"A girl doesn't have to think about what she knows."

Johnny gets a chuckle out of that. Then he turns to Mona and just stares at her.

She smiles. "I guess the power's really out, huh?"

At Mona's lame attempt to make small talk, Johnny pulls the dagger's tip out of the table, stabs it down in a new spot, and goes back to leaning on the hilt. He yawns and rubs that tired spot between his eyes.

"Power's out," he says.

"I guess Rodney will have it back on soon."

"Yeah. I guess he will."

We sit in silence. I feel a fresh trickle of blood on my skin.

Mona says to Johnny, "Baby, you look tense. Wouldn't you like me to send Susan Anne and the baby on their way now? I could give you a nice hot bath and a massage, then tuck you in for the night? Would you like that?"

Mona starts to stand up, but Johnny stabs the table again hard, so she sits, hands in her lap.

I say, "Welp, I should be going."

"Shut up," Johnny says. Which I expected.

Mona takes a big chance and leans forward to strokehis hair back from where it's fallen over his forehead and says in a voice you couldn't resist, "Johnny, what's wrong?"

"Michael."

"You miss him?"

"No."

"What then?"

"You and him . . ."

"But, Johnny . . . I swear, there never was anything . . ."

"You're lying. You and Michael fucked me while you were fucking each other. You fucked my trust. You fucked my plans. Under my own roof. My roof."

He pushes her hand away. He's crying actual tears. Mr. Big Boss. Mr. Always Get What I Want fell hook, line, and sinker for Mona's game, and now it's breaking his heart. But regardless of what he thinks she's putting him through, Mona will concentrate on what's good for her. She'll keep right on playing.

She does. She says, "No. No. Why would I lie? I love you."

Johnny wipes his face and leans his cheek on the knife handle as he looks over at me.

"Who *are* you?"

"What do you mean?"

"I mean, why are you here? What the hell do you want?" He suddenly lifts his head. His drooping eyes snap wide open. "Oh, I get it. You were helping them."

"Who?" I ask.

"These two." He pulls the blade out of the table and points it at Mona and at some vacant spot in midair that I assume means Michael's ghost. His two-and-two together is equaling five.

"Whoa now," I say. "You've got things all wrong."

"Have I?"

"Yes, you do," Mona says. "You've got to believe me."

"I don't have to do nothing."

"Johnny, you may think what you will about Michael and me, but Susan Anne had no part in it. She is my friend, that's all. An old, dear friend."

"Dear," Johnny smirks at me.

Looks to me like he's made up his mind about all of us, and no way is he going to unmake it. Mona's prime lie – the one that started this all – has left us standing in quicksand and sinking fast.

Mona brings her face closer to Johnny's, looks him right in the eye and puts her hands on each side of his wet face. She's still handling this. She's playing it out.

Without flinching, she changes the subject to an area she can command. Mona says, "Darling, what more can I say to make you understand there was never, ever anything between Michael and me?"

"You lie."

"I don't. I love you."

"Lie."

"Johnny, stop this. This is crazy."

I wish she hadn't said that.

Johnny's whole face contracts into a snarl. He dives over the table and grabs Mona's beautiful throat. She chokes and gurgles, claws at his hands. I jump onto his back, grab two handsful of his hair and pull, and we all three fall on the floor. His grip on Mona's neck and the knife comes loose. She dives back across the table and comes up with the dagger. I've still got Johnny by the hair, but I'm under him on my back. He rolls over. Now I'm on top of him like a bronc rider and banging his head on the floor, on the table, anything hard.

"Run, Mona!" I scream before, in one shrug, he throws me off, and I land on the floor between the coffee table and the couch.

Good thing she's got the layout of the house down pat. I hear her sprint for Pioche's room and the door locking behind her. Johnny's struggling to get up and run after her by the time I untangle myself from my fall. I climb onto the table and jump back on him, one arm around his neck, the other hand wrapped in his hair. He's swatting at me as he struggles forward. He trips and falls with me to his knees, where I see a reflection on a brick-sized piece of quartz crystal in arm's reach. I snag it and go to work on his handsome head. He collapses under me, and I smack him a couple more good ones to buy some time. He's definitely not the kind of guy you can hurt much by banging on his head.

I take off for Pioche's room, stubbing every toe I have and bouncing off walls. And, you know, cussing.

I pound on the door. "It's me!" I yell.

Mona unlocks the door and pulls me in, locks it behind me.

"Still got that knife?" I ask.

She holds it out to me.

"What else you got?"

Mona sifts through a bag with pink giraffes and purple monkeys on it and comes up with a .22 Derringer.

"A pop-gun. What?"

"It's the baby's," she says.

I give her the dirtiest look I can manage and check to see if the thing is at least loaded. It is. Yay, Mona.

I open Pioche's window, shove out the screen, and start tossing the kid's stuff out on the driveway.

"Out!" I yell. "NOW!"

Mona climbs through the window. I hand her the baby.

"Put as much of that crap as you can in my car, then get the fuck out of here."

This would be where she'd say, "What about you?", but she doesn't. It's so dark out there.

"Where's your car?" she whispers.

"It's . . . ah, shit . . . I can't tell."

"Come here," I say. I put my lighter directly in her hand. "It has plenty of chrome. Shouldn't be hard."

I close the window. She's on her own. Unfortunately, so am I.

I ease the door open a crack. Johnny's lurching toward me with both arms out like a Frankenstein monster. And just to add dramatic flair, he's backlit by a new quality of firelight coming from something burning in the living room that ain't just the fancy gas fireplace. Whatever it is is accompanied by gobs of smoke. The firefighter's daughter says this is not good.

As far as I'm concerned, Johnny's not coming one step closer to me, but I'll be careful choosing my moment, given my lack of firepower. Two bullets and a dagger. I hate these odds.

I wait. I sweat. Blood trickles down my neck. I take aim. Oh sweet, he falls over his own feet. I take off down the hall to the pool, go in as quiet as a little mousie, and lock the door. I hear him yell, "Fuck!" from Pioche's room. I'm not sure he's heard me.

I hear him start checking rooms, fumbling in the dark. Hoping I'm at the shallow end of the pool, I take my boots and socks off and slip into the water. Shallow end. Bonus. I feel around with my toes to try to find the Python. I hate water. I hate swimming. I'm a desert rat through and through. I'm the kind of person you'd have to throw a bucket of dust at to revive me if I got struck by more than a dozen raindrops at once. Water. Nasty stuff. But I know my old friend is in here somewhere, poor thing. Johnny didn't toss it; it slid off the edge. Should be right about . . .

Found it! Now all I need to do is keep my foot on it and dunk. Yuck! I lay the dagger on the side of the pool, hold my nose, and plunge. The chlorine burns the cuts on my neck. Did I mention I hate water?

I come up with my precious baby, lay her gently on dry land, and climb out of that horrible substance. I have no time to wring myself out when I hear Johnny try the door. As master of the house, I'm pretty sure he has all the keys. I quietly gather my belongings and slog up the dark stairs to the game room, where you'd never catch me without an arsenal. Which, as you know, I don't have.

Shit.

Chapter 20

Hide and seek. Cowboys and Indians. Cops and robbers.
Mona and Flack. We were each other's best teachers. She was
always the bad guy – her choice. I had to be the good guy.
Even if our tactics were similar, and I didn't always win.
Sometimes I wouldn't even know we were playing. Mona
would just vanish. I'd swear I was looking right at her and
poof. Gone. The invisible girl. I know she just let me find her
because she could stay gone for days at a time. I figured she
would finally get bored and need my attention. She'd pop up
in the weirdest places: under my bed, in line behind Mom and
me at the grocery store, riding her bike toward me down the
sidewalk in front of someone else's house. Random. The chick
was random. She won more than I did, but when I did get to
her first I wouldn't let her live it down until the next time she
got the best of me. She never returned the favor of humiliating
me the way I did her. It seemed to be enough for her to
succeed and move on. Pure class.

One time we were wandering around downtown near
Harold's Club looking for change that the tour bus gamblers
from California were constantly slopping out of their giant
plastic cups of slot winnings as they hunt along Virginia Street

looking for the next loose machine they knew they'd win big on. Their black fingers, green eye shade visors, white hair, and pastel pedal pushers were everywhere — like their nickels. We never failed to make a decent haul in a couple of idle hours. Our piggy banks were bursting all summer. Winter? That was a problem. The snow and freezing cold wouldn't keep them away. Oh no. The problem for us was that they'd hole up in the Mapes or Harrah's or the Riverside — the casino/hotels that offered packaged deals on cut-rate rooms, bus fare, and a happy pile of free drink tokes and Lucky Bucks to get them started. They'd arrive all bursting with merriment and enthusiasm for their three-day bender and leave mostly sullen and hungover and broke. The problem for Mona and me was that once our pigeons were inside their neon and chrome roost, we couldn't harvest their droppings without exercising significant stealth to avoid the security guards and other pesky casino staff. Sure, sneaking in and grubbing under the slot machines among the cigarette butts, used cocktail napkins, and crumpled Keno tickets for our daily bread was easier for Mona than for me, the sneak, but I tried. Eventually I was made lookout. We had a series of signals: nods, sneezes, crying about being lost (a really good one that got plenty of attention). I had to keep a sharp eye out for security, and in doing my "job," I learned the chops that eventually landed me the ultra-security gig at the Desert Diamond.

Anyway, this one time we were wandering around in front of Harold's looking for coins when I found a twenty dollar bill! Jackpot! Bingo! I looked around for Mona to celebrate my good luck, and she, of course, was nowhere in sight. I was surrounded by tourist butts — a lone kid on the sidewalk with a bunch of money in her hand. I bent down like I was tying my shoe, slipped the dough into my tennie, and went on down the street whistling like they do on cartoons when they're trying to be nonchalant. When I got to the corner at Washington

Street, I turned right and sprinted. Crossed Center Street, still sprinting. Commercial Row, running out of steam. Wells Avenue, panting and slowed to a walk, remembering to wonder where Mona split to.

"Boo!" she yelled, jumping out of the doorway of the Great Buy Liquor Store.

Scared me out of my skin.

"Dammit!" I yelled back and shoved her.

A little bit too hard. She fell backward and conked her head, hard, on the front window where a neon sign flashed Hamm's even in the daytime. The window rattled like thunder, and Mona dropped on her side unconscious.

"Mona!"

The store clerk, a great fat lady with a peroxide bouffant, pink cateye glasses with rhinestones, enough aquamarine eyeshadow to blind you, and chewing gum a mile a minute came out the door to see what all the commotion was about.

"Oh, hell!" she screamed. "Oh, Lordy hell!"

Mona had not budged.

"I'll call an ambulance!" She whirled around and went back inside.

"Mona," I said. I started patting her hands like I'd seen on t.v., not knowing what else to do. "Mona, please don't die. Please don't be dead."

But she looked kind of dead. Ghostly white. Eyes shut. I could hear the siren coming. Should I stay or run? Was I going to jail for murdering my friend? Was that blob of a lady going to finger me?

Blondie came back with a wet rag and put it on Mona's forehead.

"No blood," she said.

"Is that good?" I said.

"Dunno." She kept mopping Mona's head and muttering, "Jesus," over and over.

Apparently Jesus listened because Mona opened her eyes, crossed and weird looking.

"Wha happen?" she said.

"I . . . you passed out," I said.

Blondie said, "I heard this big boom, and when I came out, there you were. Like . . . out."

Since it seemed like Blondie didn't know how Mona came to be unconscious, I thought it best to say nothing incriminating.

"Yeah," I said. "Out."

Mona sat up. "I feel okay now." She rolled her head and shook it. We helped her stand.

"I called the ambulance. They'll be here any second."

"Yeah, Mo, you should probably sit back down before you fall down again."

Her eyes flashed with good health and determination. "Are you KIDDING me? I'm not going nowhere in no fucking ambulance!"

We were eight then. She picked up cussing early.

We could see the flashing light about two blocks away.

"Come on, let's get out of here."

"But what if you're hurt?" I said, panicking.

"What if I am? I said I ain't going nowhere in no ambulance."

She grabbed me by the arm and pulled me at a full run. Blondie called after us to stop! stop!

We never saw the ambulance arrive; we were zigging and zagging through empty lots and alleys and across the train tracks. She was like possessed. Just kept running and I just kept up with her. Barely.

Finally, we reached the shade of some cottonwoods in a crummy vacant lot and sat down on a pile of old tires to rest. I could barely breathe. My mouth was dry as a bone. Mona was gulping air like a fish.

"You sure you're okay?" I asked with my first full breath. She nodded.

"Cuz your mom is going to kill me if I let you die."

We started laughing til we ended up coughing. Then a kind of long silence happened.

Mona said, "You don't come back from an ambulance ride. You just don't. I know that for a fact."

The look on her face told me for whatever reason she had to say that, it was none of my business and to take her word for it. She picked up an empty beer bottle and threw it across the sand and tumbleweeds where it hit and shattered.

"Hey," she said, smiling her sneaky Mona smile, "I got you good, huh?"

"Uh, yeah, you sure did."

To this day she's the most evasive person I ever met.

To this day I've never told her it was me who knocked her out.

Chapter 21

It's quiet out here. House. Outside. Dead still. Crickets and frogs excluded. I'm hoping Mona and Pioche have beat feet for the bright lights of Reno and safety. I'm hoping Rodney will get the lights back on. I'm hoping Johnny . . . what? Ran off with Mona and the kid? Died of the beating I gave him with the rock? Is sitting in the dark waiting for me? Damn likely. My eyes are a bit more accustomed to the dark now. I can see some edges, the difference between solid walls and windows. The indoor pool is surrounded by glass. Come to think of it, this is a real-live glass house. Must be a bitch to keep warm in the winter. But what does Johnny care? It's only money.

I walk through the maze of grownup games, crack open the door a squidge. I'm not expecting to hear much or see much for that matter. I do, however, smell smoke. Never a good sign. A fireman's daughter knows that you're better off down low if there's smoke around. It tends to rise and float. Lucky I'm short. I make my way down the stairs.

Way too quiet.

Instead of going back into the hallway where I last saw Johnny, I choose to feel my way along one of the walls in the pool room. Somewhere there has to be a door to the outside. I push on the glass as I move along until a section budges sideways. I slowly, slowly slide it open enough to squeeze through to the outside.

I keep to the perimeter of the house, Python leading. Though it might not be a great idea, I'm thinking that restoring the power has to be my next move.

"Hey Rodney," I whisper. "Rodney." No reply, like I expected. He could be hiding out, waiting for me – which is a problem. Could be dead, which isn't. The term "bodyguard" is smack dab in the front of my mind as I remind myself where Rodney's loyalties lie.

I can see the dark powerlines silhouetted against the Milky Way. Up is about the only direction that's light at all. The breaker box will be at the end of this trail, which is looking to be right about here. I'm no expert, but I think if I push this big lever on the outside up . . .

That's all it took. The few lights that were on in the house when I got here fire up. Then there's the actual fire, now looking more like a smolder and smelling like roasted dead animal. A rug? A person? Not my problem. There is nothing and no one I need in there. I'm better off out here with room to move.

I follow another barely visible overhead line that takes me in the direction of Duke the chauffeur's cave. Smiley's place is unlocked. I feel around on the wall inside for a switch and turn on a shockingly bright bank of outdoor floodlights. Which I immediately shut off. What I did see in that split second of illumination was a full basketball court painted on the pavement and my car parked right where I left it.

Shit. This can't be good.

Still no sign of the boys.

What the heck?

I need a light. Which also reminds me I could use a cigarette. As much grass as Smiley smokes, there are bound to be lighters on every flat surface. I pat down the table in the entry way and find one. Flicking my Bic I head to the bathroom for some first aid.

The cut on my neck is jagged and not seeping as much now. The medicine cabinet is the usual man-desert of toothpaste, aspirin, and Mennen Speed Stick. No shaving cream for Mr. Natural. No help there.

With the lights back on I can see Johnny in the living room with a fire extinguisher, putting out whatever's stinking up the place. He tosses the empty cannister aside and starts pacing. The lights come up on the basketball court again. He comes out of the house, goes over to my car, looks in through the driver's side window, opens the door . . .

. . . and brings out Pioche, fast asleep.

He's looking everywhere around him like Mona's going to jump out of the sagebrush and grab the kid. He backs across the court, turns, and runs back inside. He must have gotten the now-you-see-me/now-you-don't treatment from Mona enough times to know she could be anywhere.

Johnny has turned on just about every light in the front part of the house now. What can I say? It makes me feel better to get to spy on *him*. A dim light goes on in Pioche's room. When he comes back out he's without the kid. I'm expecting Mona to jump him any moment, and I can tell he's expecting her, too. And Rodney? Still no sign of him.

Time to make the call to the police. I pre-compose the tale that Gladys Newbury will want to tell. Break-in in progress. Possible casualties. Endangered baby. Blah. Blah. Short, sweet, and as empty of details as I can make it.

I pick up Smiley's phone and tell a complete stranger at the station my name's Gladys Newbury, give them directions to the house and my schpeel. The man on the other end, a Sergeant Taylor with a voice like a radio announcer, tells me to stay calm, stay put, don't touch anything, and they'll be out as quickly as they can. Of course.

Gotta get that baby, though, and get her quick.

I made a commitment to Mona that I will keep, hell, high water, or bloodhounds. And that thought stops me cold: these Hong Kong people — that's what I've come to call whoever it is I'm supposed to turn the kid over to. The sheet of instructions Mona gave me are in the glove box, and I'm on autopilot: Take Pioche to San Francisco. Hand her over to strangers. Mona clearly intended not to show herself, but why? All I can do is keep my word. I guess San Francisco — as much as I hate it — is far enough away and big enough and weird enough that Pioche and me can be two more needles in a peace-and-love, tie-dyed haystack while I make up my mind about "these Hong Kong people."

Time's a-wasting, Flack. Get the kid and vamoose.

I grab a flashlight — one of those humongous, four D-cell mamas the cops also use as billy clubs — and go hunting for a back door. Doesn't seem like all that good a plan to just walk across the basketball court, ring the doorbell, and ask Johnny how it's hanging. This is going to take some finesse. Not my strong suit.

Let's see. Come around the back. Stick close to the wall. Flashlight, check. Python, check. Turn the corner. I hear the slider open on the deck, and Johnny steps out. Little closer, little closer. I beam the flashlight out over the sagebrush.

"Mona?" he asks the darkness.

"BOO!" I yell, holding the light under my chin to make my face real scary. Johnny whirls around and comes face to face with the Python. Well, knees to face, anyway. I walk up the four steps toward him. He wisely has his hands up.

"Where is she?" he asks with his smirk restored.

"That's for me to know and you to find out. Where's Rodney?"

I knew I'd just get an icier smirk.

"Seems like your posse is M.I.A," I say.

He laughs. "Not Rodney. He's . . ." He brings a hand down and slashes his fingers across his neck. Oh man, I liked Rodney. He was probably the only real good guy Johnny ever knew. I level the .357 at Johnny's head. He's really pissing me off now.

"Where's Mona?" he has the nerve to ask again.

"I know you've got the baby."

"Yeah, so what?"

"But you misplaced Mommie? Pretty sloppy parenting."

"Fuck you."

"Oh, sure, that's what they all say."

I've been stepping steadily toward him, blinding him with the flashlight, and keeping my gun steady.

"Awful big gun for such a little girl. Ain't your arm getting tired?"

Hate to say that it is, but I can't give him the satisfaction. I'll keep this up all night.

"Tell you what," Johnny says, "how about we go inside, have a drink, talk over old times. . ."

Right then we hear the siren. The cavalry's coming. We both flinch, looking in the direction of sound. And he's quicker than I am at getting my attention back on the job at hand. He's on me in a split second, my gun goes sailing off the deck into the darkness. I drop the flashlight. Then I do something I'm unaccustomed to doing: I go limp. I surrender. I burst into tears. He's still holding my arms down, but clearly enjoying my pain.

"She was my best friend . . ." I wail. "I loved her so much . . ." Wah, wah, wah.

He lets my arms go, still sitting across me.

"Aw, ain't that sweet?"

What's sweet is the little Derringer I have tucked in my bra. I've got to be quick, and I've got two shots. I reach for the flashlight with my left hand. He reaches for it, too, giving me just enough time to grab the Derringer and pump two into his chest at pointblank range. The surprise more than the impact knocks him backward, and I spring to my feet. I fish his dagger out of my boot and finish the job with a couple of double-handed plunges. And I goddam well spit on him just for spite.

I rush inside to assess my situation. From the looks of the dust being kicked up on the road in, Reno PD has only sent the one squad car. A break-in at a prominent citizen's residence will get you lights and sirens, but not a whole lot more. I have just enough time to gather up Pioche and hunker down in my GTO til whoever they sent to restore law and order goes starts securing the premises.

Not only have they sent one car, they dispatched only one officer, who appears willing to take his sweet time. He heaves himself out of the car ,having to grab the top with one hand to haul out his bulk. As soon as he opens the front door and gets a load of the mayhem inside there's going to be all kinds of hell to pay, but he does the polite thing and rings the bell first. Pioche and I are lying on the front seat, the middle console digging a hole in my ribs. Man, can that kid sleep. I'd like to have what she's having.

The cop finally enters the house. I put the car in neutral, crack open the driver's side door, jump out, and give us a push, and we're rolling. Out from under the lights of the basketball court to the sweet freedom of darkness. A few yards down the road I fire up the engine and lights and high-tail it the hell out of here. With the dirt road in super good shape, I keep on driving fast. Got to make it to Highway 40 before more boys in blue get the s.o.s.

Once we get to 40, I have a decision to make: turn left and take that slow, windy son of a bitch over the Sierras or turn right and make my way to Interstate 80, newer, wider, and a lot straighter. I decide to turn right toward Reno and slow down to blend in with local traffic. We're all the way to town before a bunch of squad cars and firetrucks and ambulances whizz by, tearing-ass with lights and sirens blaring. They sure don't notice little ole us.

I have a hunch that enclosed in some compartment or diaper box or footie p.j.s, I will be finding a Bay-ta-max videotape. Which will only add to the shitstorm I'll be landing in after I come home from San Francisco after delivering Pioche the Hong Kong people.

You can bet I will find someone trustable to give that tape to. That's about the only positive thing I have to look forward to when I get back. A lot of people are going to want a lot of answers from me. Any way I look at it, my name as usual will be Mud. But what can I do? For now, there's just this one, last good thing to do for my old friend

Chapter 22

I stop for gas at the Shell on the corner of Fifth and Keystone. Wash the dust off of my windows. Check on the baby. I sort of hope Pioche sleeps through the whole trip—especially seeing as I'm not sure what to do with her if she doesn't. Then again I sort of hope she doesn't. It'd give me something else to think about. Maybe I could tell her some of the good stories—few as they were—about Mona and me when we were kids. She ought to know her mom. Or maybe I could tell her some lies that would help her grow up different from Mona and me. Tell her that the world is safe and that she'll never get hurt and that the people she loves will never leave her. Except her mother is . . .? Snap out of it, Flack. Maybe. Maybe. If I was the praying type, this would be the time for it, but you know how that goes. Anyhow, the kid will for sure be better off without me, without all of this: this town, these people.

I take a minute to snuggle Mona's pretty baby into a makeshift nest on the back seat before I turn left onto Interstate 80. This time of night—I mean, morning – I can really let'er rip. I take the speedometer up to 120. The GTO loves it. We fly over the freeway toward the Sierras. Let the crazy lights of Reno grow smaller and smaller, farther and farther back into the distance until they're gone.

THE END

. . . of this part . . .

> *Find out what–or who–gets*
> *Flack Murrow extra fired up*
> *in her next adventure,*
> **YOU MAKE ME TINGLE**

Love to hear from you! mitzimiles.author@gmail.com